From the Darkness

Scary Short Stories

Jordan Grupe

Manor House

Library and Archives Canada
Cataloguing in Publication

Title: From the Darkness : scary short stories / Jordan Grupe.
Names: Grupe, Jordan, author.
Identifiers: Canadiana 20230572340 |
ISBN 9781998938063 (softcover)
ISBN 978-1-998938-07-0 (hardcover)
Subjects: LCGFT: Short stories. | LCGFT: Horror fiction.
Classification: LCC PS8613.R88 F76 2023 |
DDC C813/.6—dc23

Note: This collection of short stories is a work of fiction. Any resemblance to locations or persons alive or dead is purely coincidental.

First Edition
Cover Design-layout / Interior- layout: Michael Davie
198 pages / 51,760 words. All rights reserved.
Published 2023 / Copyright 2023
Manor House Publishing Inc.
452 Cottingham Crescent, Ancaster, ON, L9G 3V6
www.manor-house-publishing.com (905) 648-4797

Funded by the Government of Canada | **Canadä**

For Nolan: Thanks for showing me the good shit.

Acknowledgements

First, my thanks to you the reader - this book wouldn't be possible without you.

Many thanks as well to my mom, Vanessa. You are a constant inspiration to me.   Your kindness and generosity do not go unnoticed by me or the rest of the world. I'm in awe of you. Thank you again for your endless encouragement, and so much more.

Sincere thanks to Mike Davie and Manor House for publishing this book and my prior books, including my debut novel ***Beneath the Asylum***, and my follow-up novel ***Escape from the Asylum***, plus ***No Sleep Tonight*** collection of short stories (and now my latest collection of short stories: ***From the Darkness***), fulfilling a lifelong dream of seeing my work in print - I really can't thank you enough for taking a chance on this upstart Internet writer. Thanks also to Ryan Davie and the rest of the family. I love you all.

Thanks also to Nolan, my brother. When I write you're almost always my imaginary reader. You did what all good older brothers do, you showed me the good shit. Kurt Vonnegut, Joe Hill, Nick Cutter, etc. Thanks for having great taste. Hope you liked this one too. Thank you to all my friends and family as well for supporting me in my writing. I love you all.

- **Jordan Grupe**

Table of Contents

Reviews for *From the Darkness* and prior books:

"Jordan Grupe is one of the most unique voices of modern horror. His style's fresh and his ideas differ from what one's used to in horror. If you want to be scared, disturbed, but most of all surprised, give this collection a try. You won't regret it!"
- **Rene Rehn**, Author, *The First Few Times Always Hurt*

"Frightening, funny, and thoroughly twisted. Once again, Grupe's collection checks all the boxes."
- **Jesse Pullins** Author, *The Paper Mache Man*

"His imagination is boundless. A trailblazer. Horror has a new master, and its name is Jordan Grupe.
 - **Marcus Starr**, Author, *Nora's Curse* and *Monsters in the Moonlight*

"Despite being a relatively new addition to the horror writing scene, Jordan Grupe has made a name for himself as an excellent storyteller. His ability to build characters and terrify readers is consistently impressive as he continues to produce high quality horror content. I have featured a few of his tales on my YouTube channel "Mr. Creeps" and the response has always been amazing!"
- **Mr. Creeps** (683,000-subscribers on YouTube)

"Jordan has a knack for making the mundane menacing (I'll never look at garden gnomes the same way again). His stories are immersive, dragging the reader in kicking and screaming, with just enough humor to help wash down the absolute dread you experience when visiting his wicked worlds."

- **Travis Brown** (Grand_Theft_Motto on Reddit No Sleep), author, *House with One Hundred Doors*

About the Author:

Jordan Grupe is the critically acclaimed author of *Beneath the Asylum* and its highly anticipated follow-up novel, *Escape from the Asylum*. *From the Darkness* is his second collection of horror short stories, following *No Sleep Tonight*, a short horror anthology.

His YouTube channel: *Jordan Grupe Horror* is a fast-growing source for short horror narrations, some of which have garnered over 100,000 views. He is the author of more than 250 short stories, many of which have appeared on popular podcasts and YouTube horror channels internationally.

His writings are often shared with a vast audience in the hundreds of thousands via the websites Reddit.com (under profile Jgrupe) and YouTube as well as author website: JordanGrupe.com. The author and his works are also featured on an array of other websites, including amazon.com and other Amazon sites; the websites of other major books retailers and the publisher's website: www.manor-house-publishing.com.

From the Darkness. author Jordan Grupe's fourth book and latest collection of scary short stories, is certain to please his growing audience and further establish him as a major writer of psychologically disturbing tales of fear and intrigue.

Beneath the Asylum - his breakthrough first novel - drew its inspiration from the author's own experience as a security guard at a psychiatric hospital with a dilapidated, and reportedly haunted, old mansion on its grounds. This would lead to his follow-up second novel *Escape from the Asylum*, bringing readers deeper into a dark realm of gripping horror.

No Sleep Tonight continued the author's tales of horror with his first collection of truly scary short stories. And now we have *From the Darkness* – his newest collection of outstanding short stories, further entrenching his reputation as a leading writer of gripping horror stories.

The Tiger's Crown

It was just before recess when Zach asked me to hold his egg. We were doing a school project where the goal was to keep an egg safe for an entire week, as if it were your own baby. If you dropped your egg and broke it, you got an F.

Mr. Marco had signed all of the eggs with a Sharpie, so there was no chance of cheating. Everyone in class had devised a plan to keep their prized egg safe for the week, and Zach was no exception. He was using a white and red thermos lined with tissue paper inside. It looked secure, and I wasn't worried about breaking it. In fact, it looked safer than mine, and I was starting to consider changing my design.

Maybe because I was distracted thinking about my own egg container device, I didn't have a firm enough grip on Zach's thermos. When I got bumped from behind by another kid I fumbled it.

The whole contraption went flying and landed right in front of the teacher's desk. Mr. Marco saw the egg jump from the thermos and a second later it went SPLAT, right on the floor in front of his desk.

"Jason! Was that your egg?" he demanded, leaping up from his chair.

Mr. Marco had always hated me. I had him in the sixth grade, after he replaced the best teacher in school at the last minute. Then in the eighth grade, he surprised me again by replacing the second best teacher in school and taking over for his class which I was entering. The first day I couldn't believe it, seeing Mr. Marco sitting behind the desk where Mr. L was supposed to be sitting. Mr. L was my older brother's favorite teacher ever. Three years prior I'd heard all the stories of how he'd taken his students on field trips every month and entertained them with his comedic lectures, using characters and voices and props that captivated even the most "unteachable" students.

Mr. Marco, by contrast, was a Phys Ed major who thought gym class was superior to everything and barely understood math or science. He was highly favored among the jocks and bullies and despised by the geeks and nerds, like myself.

That first day of eighth grade, Mr. Marco was sitting up front, and he must have seen the disappointed look on my face, because he scowled at me and yelled at me to take my seat. It was as if he had read my mind, and knew I hated him, and that I was disappointed he was my teacher again.

For almost two full years I'd suffered under Mr. Marco. He was mean, rude, and somehow managed to become friends with all of the bullies in school who regularly beat me up during recess. One of those bullies was Zach, whose egg I had just broken.

"No, Mr. Marco," I said, showing him *my* egg, safe and sound. "That was Zach's."

I turned around and looked at Zach, then wished I hadn't.

"Sorry," I mumbled under my breath.

The teacher's face went a shade redder. Zach was his favorite student. Zach was the quarterback on the football team which Mr. Marco coached. And Zach, despite being the worst student in class, was adored by Mr. Marco.

The teacher's eyes shifted and I saw he was looking at Zach sympathetically - Zach, who was standing behind me, vibrating with rage. The freckles on his cheeks became harder to see, as his entire face went crimson.

Despite the fact that I knew he wanted to fail me, a precedent had already been set and everyone knew what had to happen next.

"Unless that was a decoy, you get an F, Zach," Mr. Marco said, sitting back down and marking something in his notebook with a red pen. "Next time pick a smarter person to hold your baby."

Somehow that stung worse than anything yet.

*

It didn't take long for Zach to find me during recess.

His tall, lanky, hyena-voiced friend Chris accompanied him as they held me up against a wall and began to lay a beating on me. It didn't help that Zach now had both hands free, while I had to hold onto my precious egg for dear life.

Zach punched my arm again and again, giving me a Charlie Horse that would last for weeks.

At first I didn't protest. I felt like I deserved it. But then it started to hurt worse and worse and I needed to get away more than anything. It felt like something in my arm was about to rupture or break or worse. But no matter how hard I struggled, the two larger, stronger boys held me in place.

Finally, after what felt like hours, I could take no more, and crumpled to the ground, curling into a ball, still trying to protect my egg.

Zach said some parting words, which I barely heard, no longer caring what he thought of me. Once upon a time we'd been friends. I'd gone to his house and gone to his birthday parties. But that felt like a different lifetime. A century ago, in another universe.

*

I walked home from school feeling crushed and weak, wincing every time someone ran past me on the sidewalk, thinking it might be Zach coming to lay another beating on me. Looking over my shoulder again and again, I had a feeling he would be coming for me. What he'd done to me at recess wasn't enough. It would never be enough.

When I glanced back I saw him running down the sidewalk trying to catch up with me. I pretended not to notice, then when I went around the next corner I began to run.

A few seconds later I looked back to see he had several of his friends from the hockey team with him. They were running full-tilt, laughing and screaming at me as I ran away. Their threats made me certain that if they caught me they would hurt me worse than I'd ever been hurt before. And I really wanted to avoid that.

I turned onto a path, leaving the road, racing towards the forest. Immediately I regretted the decision, knowing that I was headed towards an even more secluded area, far away from the relative safety of city streets and plenty of witnesses.

But it was too late to turn back now. The bullies were right behind me, gaining on me fast. I threw my backpack to the ground, trying to gain any advantage I could, and heard one of them tumble to the ground when they tripped over it.

"I'll kill you for that," I heard him yelling after me, but I didn't look back.

By the time I got to the forest I realized they weren't right behind me anymore. They were still trailing me, but at a jogging pace now. And they were pulling binders and school books out of my backpack and scattering them everywhere as they walked.

"Man, you really shouldn't litter," Zach was saying, joined by jeers and laughter from the others. "All this stuff has your name on it, you should really come back and pick it up! Look, there goes your math textbook, that's gotta be worth like fifty bucks, right?"

I winced, hearing him tear pages from it as they followed me into the forest. It probably cost more than a hundred dollars, I thought, which I'd have to pay back after the school year ended. Either way, I wasn't turning around for the backpack. I would take my life over my school books any day.

The path was too obvious, I realized. Knowing I had temporarily lost them in the trees, I decided to veer off from it. I had to get creative if I wanted to lose them.

So I went off the path and ran through some bushes, heading away from the trail.

It didn't take long for them to notice, and I heard them crunching through leaves as they followed after me a few seconds later.

"I SEE YOU!" Zach shouted, and I looked back and saw he was pointing right at me. "And I'm gonna fucking KILL YOU!"

It was an accident, I wanted to scream. But it wouldn't make a difference. None of it mattered to him. He just wanted blood.

Running as fast as I could through the fallen leaves, I tripped over a branch. It was hidden by the rusted brown and yellow foliage and so I hadn't seen it.

When I looked up, I realized there was a hiding place just beside me that I would not have noticed if not for tripping.

A large, hollowed-out log was to my right, and I crawled inside of it.

It was large enough for me to fit inside, but just barely. I held my breath, hearing the sounds of footsteps coming closer. The other boys were right outside, looking for me.

"He was here a second ago," one of them said. "I saw him."

Patiently I waited for them to leave, hoping they wouldn't linger too long. The log was wet beneath my ass and I felt the rotten moisture leaking through my pants. I noticed movement to my right and looked to see a fat spider crawling on the ceiling of my hiding spot, and just beyond there were millipedes, potato bugs, and little red worms which squirmed and wriggled as they poked their heads from the decaying wood. There were probably more of them beneath me, and I realized I felt movement under me. The entire rotten log was alive with insects and creepy-crawlies.

Horrified and sick to my stomach, I nearly burst out of there, screaming. But I stayed where I was and hoped they would leave. Instead, they lingered nearby, far too close for comfort.

"Is he in there?" I heard one of them ask.

With fear overwhelming my revulsion, I set down my precious egg and clambered further into the decaying log. I crawled through thick spider webs as things skittered down my back and into my pants, biting back a scream and forcing myself to continue onward. All the way to the end, or at least, what I thought was the end of the hollow log.

Instead of bumping up against a rock or roots or cold hard ground, I kept crawling. Into the darkest place I'd ever been.

Something about it was calling to me, even more than my sense of curiosity at this strange world which seemed to be opening up all around me.

I sensed by the noise of my movements that I was now in a wide open space, damp and cold like a cave, and I felt around, realizing I could stand up now. I sensed there was something just ahead of me, and I reached out to feel a smooth wooden surface.

My hand probed the flat surface for any marker or indication of what it might be, and suddenly I felt something round and polished jutting out from it.

For a few seconds I couldn't figure it out, because the context clues were all wrong. Whatever this was didn't belong here. It belonged in a house, not a cave beneath the forest.

It was a door knob.

Which meant this was a door.

But where could it possibly lead to?

I decided to take my chances with whatever was on the other side, rather than risking another confrontation with Zach and his friends.

My heart was pounding fast as I turned the handle, deciding to take a chance and explore further in this strange place. Maybe it was a hobbit's hole, my young mind thought. Or the home of a leprechaun.

As I stepped through, into another world, I forgot all about Zach and the other boys who were looking to beat me up.

As the door swung open I was hit by a blast of cold air, much more chilly than the damp basement feeling of the cave I had just been in. This new place was in the middle of winter, and it was full of blowing snow, whereas the place I'd just come from was relatively warm. I was wearing jeans and a hoodie, and I was immediately freezing cold and shivering.

"Whoa," I exclaimed, unable to stop myself from wandering forward.

Scared of going too far from the door, I hesitantly began to explore this new place.

I pushed my way out through thick fir trees, and eventually found myself in a clearing, surrounded by forest. It was dim outside, but it was daylight. The sky overhead was obscured by thick, swirling gray clouds which dumped snow down constantly. My feet were instantly soaked and freezing cold, since my running shoes were not made for this sort of weather.

Clutching myself and rubbing my arms to regain some warmth, I decided this was too much to bear. I was about to turn back, but then I heard the sound of tiny bells jingling, and a voice speaking to me from nearby. It was a woman's voice, soft and sweet, like music to my ears.

"Oh, dear boy," she said, emerging from behind a tree. Her hair was dark and she was dressed in gray robes, the same color as the clouds, covered in little silver bells. "How did you find yourself stranded in the forests of Hollow's End?"

Part of me wanted to turn and run, but her smile was warm and friendly, and the tinkling bells reminded me of Christmas, so I found myself staying.

"Oh, hello. Nice to meet you. Actually, I'm not stranded. There's a door back there. I found this place by accident and…

Brrrrr, it's beautiful… but cold! I think I'll have to be heading back now."

She came a little closer and I saw she was very pretty. Her face looked like it belonged to a supermodel or a famous actress whose name I couldn't place, and I found myself staring at her intently, despite my desire to go back to where I'd come from where it was warmer.

Then, before I knew it, she was standing right in front of me.

"If you're cold, I can get you a coat. And some hot cocoa. Would you like that?"

I felt myself nodding, and she took my hand in her own freezing cold one, and when she touched me my entire body became covered with goosebumps, and I found myself going with her. She led me away from the door I'd come in through, and deeper into the cold and wintery world of Hollow's End.

*

A little while later we were sitting inside someplace warm, although I didn't remember walking there. I had a fur coat around my shoulders and I was sipping cocoa, staring at the beautiful woman across from me. She was old enough to be my teacher, and it should have felt rude, but I couldn't tear my eyes away. And she didn't say anything, only looked at me with that same warm smile.

But then her happy expression dropped and she looked away, as a tear dripped down her cheek, spilling to the floor, where it immediately froze solid. Her lower lip quivered as she said a silent apology to me.

"What's wrong," I asked.

"Nothing," she said. "How's your hot chocolate?"

"Delicious!"

And it was. The best I'd ever tasted.

"Are you hungry?" she asked, wiping away the tears which had turned to snowflakes on her face.

"Yes, I'm very hungry," I replied. I couldn't help it, I was starving. My stomach was rumbling and I felt like dinner should have been hours ago, and yet time was funny here. I wasn't entirely sure how long I'd been in this world, on the other side of the door. But the groans from my belly were saying it had been a long time.

"What is your favorite thing in the world to eat?"

I thought about this for a second, and it didn't take long to come up with an answer.

"My mom's beef stew," I said. "It's the best!"

Her face lit up in a warm grin again and she got up and went to the stove. I noticed for the first time there was a black pot simmering there.

"Well, what do you know? That's exactly what I'm making for dinner tonight. Beef stew!"

My mouth started watering at the smell. It was exactly like what I remembered from home. Which reminded me I should be going back there. My mom would be worried about me.

Something about this was creeping me out too, the more I thought about home and about the strange situation I was in. Images of Hansel and Gretel crossed my mind, although I hadn't yet labeled this woman with the dreaded "W" word. I didn't think she'd like it if I called her that, even if it was true.

As I was about to open my mouth to say I had to leave, she presented me with a steaming bowl filled with beef stew, and I forgot what I had been thinking about. The dish looked just like my mom's, and the smell was overwhelming. Next she set down a board with a freshly-baked loaf of bread sitting atop it, steaming and warm with butter ready for spreading.

I couldn't possibly leave right after she'd done all this for me, I thought to myself, and began to dig in.

The meat was tender, the broth perfectly thick and seasoned, and the carrots, potatoes, and onions had just the right amount of bite. It was the best beef stew I'd ever eaten - peppery and hot - and I quickly downed two bowls, devouring four slices of warm, crunchy fresh bread slathered in salted butter, which I used to mop up the puddles at the bottom of the bowl.

Wiping my face with a napkin, I belched loudly and excused myself, my face turning red with embarrassment.

"No need to apologize. A healthy burp is a sign of a properly cooked meal, in my books," she said from across the table.

I realized then that she hadn't eaten anything, and felt bad for not noticing earlier.

"I'm just not very hungry these days," she said, as if reading my thoughts. "But I'm glad I could make you happy with a meal. The greatest joy in life is in feeding people, I always say."

"That's what my mom always says too!"

It wasn't quite what she said, but close enough.

The woman's face broke again and frozen tears began to pour from both eyes, as she let out a gut-wrenching sob.

It was startling, after our pleasant conversation so far, but obviously there was something deeply troubling this woman.

"What's wrong?" I asked. "I'm not sure if I can help, but I'd be happy to try."

"That's sweet of you to offer," she said. "But you're just a boy. I need someone… Well, someone who can be very, very sneaky. No, I'm sorry. It's too dangerous."

"What's too dangerous?" I asked, curious now.

She walked over to the fireplace and looked into the flames. Then, after some time, she began to speak.

"It's been years since I've been trapped in this place. An outcast sent to live at the edge of the forest."

Her voice was sad, and almost brought me to tears as she continued her tragic tale.

"My family once ruled this land. We were fair and just. Everyone in Hollow's End had enough to eat. It was warm and the sun was shining every day. Crops grew tall in the soil of our lands, towering to the heights of trees. There was always more than enough to go around.

"But then a great beast emerged from the forest. It was a jungle cat, large and white, and with it came the snow. The great tiger was intelligent, and could speak and enthrall the hearts of men. He convinced them to take my crown from me, and with it, I lost my power to hold back his never-ending winter. The trees went bare overnight. The crops began to wither and fail. And soon there was little to eat, and never enough to go around."

She showed me the bottom of the pot of stew, and the few scraps that remained, then set it down to rest on the stove.

"You gave me all of it?" I asked, stunned and heartbroken. "But you don't even know me."

"My mother always taught me to be kind. To help strangers lost in the cold."

I thought about this for a few moments before making an impulse decision I would come to greatly regret.

"Well, my mom taught me stuff too! And I want to help you. Just tell me what you need me to do. If you need someone to be sneaky, well, I'll be the sneakiest sneak you've ever seen. I'll get your crown back for you from that tiger!"

She smiled at me, and this time it didn't feel so warm. In fact, I felt a chill run up my spine as she began to laugh and nod, telling me, "Good boy. Very good boy."

*

I found myself outside, dressed in a thick black fur coat and boats, trudging through the snow. There was a sword in a scabbard attached to my belt, and I had a vague memory of being taught how to use it.

How much time has passed? How long did you spend learning how to use that sword? Your mother must be missing you...

Panicked thoughts ran through my mind but they were suppressed now. They were at the back. Hidden. Far away where I couldn't get to them. The only thing that was important now was the mission. Getting the crown. And I could see the glow of it in the distance, shining silver with the magic beacon cast by the (*witch, she's a witch!*) woman who was so kind and so good to me. Heading further and further away from the door which had brought me to this strange place - but that thought didn't really trouble me anymore. Now I was focused on my mission. Getting back the crown was all that mattered. The crown. *The crown.* The crown.

At some point I realized I was standing right in front of a gate. Not only that, but someone was speaking to me.

"Your NAME, sir?"

"Revere Frostborne the eighth," I answered, the strange words coming out with no conscious effort. My voice sounded deeper, I noticed, and looked down to see my hands were lined and cracked, calluses formed at the tips of my fingers from many years of hard labor - or swordplay.

"Ah, we've been expecting you for some time," the man said.

I looked him up and down and saw he was a guard dressed in a suit of armor, and there were dozens of others like him all around me. I was in a castle, like something out of Game of Thrones or Lord of the Rings. There were tapestries on the wall and flickering torches hung beside them as I was marched down a long corridor, deeper and deeper into the heart of a grand and ancient keep.

After going through numerous lines of guards, each larger and more ornately armored than the last, we finally arrived at a massive entryway. There, the guard who had been my escort left me.

I looked up at the eight new guards who stood at the doorway, far more formidable-looking than my previous escort, each dressed in gold armor fringed with red, brandishing the sharpest and most ornate-looking spears I'd ever seen. They blocked my entrance and said nothing.

For a moment I couldn't think what they could be expecting of me, but then the words came from my lips before I could consider their meaning.

"The armies of the Frostborne Giants have a proposal," I said. "I must speak to him."

The guards parted for me and I walked through their midst, entering the largest and most lavishly-decorated throne room I'd ever seen.

Sounds of clanking, rattling armor could be heard behind me and I realized the guards were escorting me the rest of the way, towards what appeared to be a huge throne in the distance.

As I got closer I realized it wasn't a person sitting on the purple throne. It was a white tiger. Much larger than any jungle cat I'd ever seen on Earth, this beast was easily three times the size of a White Bengal Tiger. And sitting atop its head was a golden crown.

THE CROWN. GET THE CROWN. YOU MUST GET THE CROWN.

The words ran through my head feverishly, running over every other consideration like a steamroller.

Once I was close enough to smell the fish on the great cat's breath, it spoke.

"Why did you come here?" it asked in a deep baritone voice which rattled my eardrums. "Do you seek to steal my crown for the Silver Witch of the forest?"

GET THE CR…

The command running through my mind was interrupted somehow, and for the first time in a long while, I could think for myself. But I wasn't sure how long it would last.

"How did you know I came for your crown?"

The guards' spears were suddenly at my throat from eight different angles, less than an inch away. My heart was pounding fast.

"I could smell her on you. Cats have much better noses than people, you know. Lower your weapons, he did not realize what he was doing. He still doesn't. The Silver Witch is cunning, you all know that."

The guards lowered their spears reluctantly.

"Blikjin, Frija, go. Ready the men for an attack. This is likely a diversion," the tiger said, and two of the guards ran off. The other six formed a defensive formation all around us.

"Frederick! Come quickly! I need your expertise."

A white haired wizard carrying a staff shuffled over and immediately began pawing at my head, as if inspecting for lice.

"Ah yes, just as I would have suspected."

He pulled something out from the back of my skull which continued to emerge for a long, long time as he yanked at it. It felt as if he were pulling a snake from my brain.

As he gathered it and looped it into a coil, the great tiger began to whisper in my ear.

"She can't hear us anymore. Now, listen closely, boy. This is what you must do…"

*

I was walking again. The cold wind was blowing in my face and the snow was stinging my skin, but I had my wits again. I could think for myself.

The King of Hollow's End devised a plan to rid the land of the witch once and for all, but it would be up to me to implement it. If I failed, she would have everything she needed to take over again. And to plunge this other world into permanent darkness.

"She's far too powerful even for me to defeat," the king told me. "But you will have the advantage. You will be able to catch her by surprise in a way none of us could."

The crown was in my hand, the snow crunching beneath my boots. There was a long road ahead of me, although I didn't remember traveling it the first time, I would be present for every moment of this leg back.

Fortunately for me, the king's throne room was imbued with a powerful magic, put in place by the wizard, Frederick. The witch wasn't aware of his power, or his presence, otherwise she wouldn't have risked sending me alone. But now I was in a place of advantage. All I had to do was get her to put on the crown and it would drain all of her magic, making her powerless, due to a hex placed upon it by the wizard. Without her magic, the witch would freeze like ice and shatter into a million pieces

I continued to walk, pondering my plan and every possible thing that could go wrong. For years, I marched through the cold and the snow, attacked by bandits some days while on others I had nothing to eat. There were good friends made along the way, enemies vanquished and companions lost to sickness and arrows. Yet somehow I managed to survive.

By the time I made it back to that frozen forest I was a changed man. No longer a boy - those days were long since forgotten. I hardly remembered how I had come to be in this place, and part of me suspected I'd lived here all along - that those previous memories were simply another hex placed upon me by the witch.

The sound of tinkling bells broke me from my thoughts, and I looked up to see her standing there, right in front of me. Only inches away.

"You're back," she said with that same smile like an eel about to eat supper. "Do you have it?"

No questions of how I was or whether I'd run into trouble. No thank you for my years - no - decades of journeying to fetch it for her.

My hands shaking with barely concealed rage, I fetched it from beneath the folds of my tattered cloak and handed it to her.

"You're shaking," she said, taking it from me. Her voice was nervous, and slightly suspicious. "Are you alright?"

"The years have done a number on me, m'lady. I am not the boy I once was. I've grown old in my quest to find this for you. And to slay the great tiger who stole your throne."

"But you have done it? He is dead?"

I nodded.

"Yes. He is dead."

Smiling wider, she began to put the crown on top of her head. Lowering it to the point where it almost rested there, it hovered for several long moments… But then she pulled it away.

"No…" she muttered. "Too easy…"

Her face was getting red with rage, and I realized she had caught me.

"You shouldn't be able to tell your own age. That was part of the spell. It was supposed to keep you blind to how much time you spent here - a variation on the hex which enchants my forest."

She raised her hand and a bolt of energy deformed the air in front of me, causing it to shimmer, and then it moved over me, enveloping me. It was pure heat. Like the air just above a fire, where you would toast your marshmallows.

I screamed as the boiling air began to melt my skin, setting my fur cloak ablaze.

"You will learn not to disobey me again," said the witch, inspecting the crown in her hands with disinterest. "But for now. Pain."

The scorching air got even hotter somehow, and my hair caught on fire a second later. Now I couldn't even scream. My voice was caught, my face frozen in a grimace of sheer agony.

Time stretched out forever, although it only lasted a few instants.

Then thankfully the burning haze was extinguished by a snowy gust of wind.

"Enough, witch! You have destroyed this poor boy's life. Now you will pay!"

It was the wizard, I realized with relief. He had come to save me. And not only that, but he was riding on the back of the great white tiger king.

Frederick leapt from his back and began to advance on the witch as the tiger flanked her from the other side. He held his staff out in front of him and cast bolts of white lightning at the witch - who in turn sent them ricocheting in every direction, deflecting them with a swirling gray cloud which she manipulated expertly.

One bolt of lightning deflected back exactly at Frederick, hitting him centermass, and sending him flying backwards. After hurtling through the air several yards, he landed against a rock, where he lay motionless.

"FREDERICK!" the tiger-king shouted, abandoning his attack and racing across the snow to his fallen friend.

The gray witch was moving towards the king, slowly closing the distance from behind, and I realized she would kill him if I didn't do something.

And then I saw the crown lying in the snow.

I would only have one chance. And I would need to be very sneaky.

"You thought you could kill me?" the witch was saying, sending a shimmering orb of heat towards the tiger-king. "You really thought you could kill ME?"

The tiger lunged at her ankle, ducking beneath the orb of magic at the last second and grabbing hold of her leg in his jaw.

"NOW!" he yelled around the bloody flesh in his mouth. "DO IT NOW!"

I didn't hesitate.

As the witch was distracted, screaming in pain, I jammed the crown on top of her head, twisting it further onto her forehead until it covered her eyes, and was impossible to remove.

It began to turn red, then white-hot, as she howled in pain and tried to pry it off. But it wouldn't budge.

The witch burst into flame, and I held my hands up to the bonfire of her body to warm myself up as I watched her turn to cinders.

*

Sadly, a few minutes after the witch died, so did Frederick, the wizard. He managed to hang on for a little while, just long enough for his magic to send the witch back to hell where she belonged, but then his injuries overcame him. He had used the most powerful magic available to him in his effort to stop the witch - and she had turned it around on him, deflecting it right back at his heart.

A tear ran down the tiger-king's cheek, and I held out my hand to stroke his soft, warm fur. His eyes were brimming with tears as he spoke.

"You should go home. Your family must be missing you."

"That was just a lie from the witch. This is my home. It always has been. The rest was just a dream."

"Come," said the tiger-king. "Let me show you something."

He led me towards a thicket of trees. Pushing a few branches aside with his great paw, he went into them, the sticky sap leaving brown smears on his white coat.

"In there," he said, pointing to a strange door, isolated in the middle of the forest. "That is where your true life lies. Looking back, one day you will think that THIS was just a dream."

Memories flooded back of my mother and father, my friends and family, and of course, the bullies who had tormented me.

"It's been so long. There's nothing left for me there."

"Time works differently in some worlds - at least that's what Frederick told me. He, himself, was from another world. And he said one day he would return there and only a few hours would have passed. Perhaps it will be the same for youu. There is only one way to find out."

I looked at him and found that now I was crying. I gave the giant tiger a hug and he lifted his paw to hug me back, retracting his enormous claws to do so.

"You are always welcome in my kingdom if you wish to return one day."

And with that, I left him behind, pushing open the door and going back into the cave on the other side.

I found myself back on Earth, and once again in the form of a boy. Unsure how much time precisely had passed, I scrambled out of the log and looked around for any sign of the bullies who had tormented me so many years ago.

Something crunched beneath my foot as I made my way out of the log, and I looked down to see it was my egg. The sacred egg which I'd been tasked with keeping safe.

It seemed so silly now.

I had a good average in all of my classes. Failing the egg project didn't mean anything, really. Except maybe for Zach, who was barely passing. Maybe he would have to be held back because of my blunder.

Suddenly I felt bad for dropping his egg, even if he had beaten me up for it. I hoped he would pass and get to graduate.

I found my backpack at the entrance to the forest, with all of my papers tossed on the grass. My math textbook was fine, though. Despite what he'd said, Zach hadn't ripped it up - he'd only torn out blank pages from a notebook. Maybe he felt bad.

After I'd gathered up my belongings, I began walking home again.

Halfway there, I looked up and saw Zach. He was on the front porch of his house, looking like he didn't really want to go inside. A man and a woman were yelling at each other loud enough to be heard from the street.

"Hey, Zach!" I called over to him.

He looked up and seemed angry for a second, but then seemed to do a double-take. He walked over to me and looked me up and down.

"What's up with you? You look different," he said.

"I've just had some time to think," I replied. "It doesn't give you an excuse to be a dick to me, but I'm sorry I smashed your egg. It was a mistake. Somebody pushed me from behind and it went flying."

"Yeah, okay," he said. "No big deal. I'm still gonna graduate. Just barely, though."

"That's good."

I thought for a second to myself.

"Hey, do you want to come hang out at my place for a bit? I've got the new Street Fighter game. And I've got some eggs and a Sharpie. After two years in his class, I've gotten pretty good at forging Mr. Marco's signature."

He smiled and nodded, and the two of us left the sounds of muffled arguments on the other side of the door and walked away down the street together.

*

This all happened many years ago. I'm in my late thirties now, and the memories of my other life in that other world have faded. But I still remember how to use a sword. And I still remember the terror I felt as the Silver Witch of Hollow's End set me on fire with her magic. That time while it consumed me felt like it was drawn out forever - and I realized over the years why that was.

In the case of the witch's magic, time does not heal all wounds. It makes little difference.

I think about that sometimes when I'm trying to fall asleep at night, tossing and turning from the unquenchable pain. In the darkness of my bedroom. Every time I see a shadow that looks vaguely like a person I'm still convinced it's her. And that she's laughing in the darkness, tormenting me with her magic.

It doesn't matter that she's dead.

Now I know that there are an infinite number of different worlds out there.

And an infinite variety of horrific things waiting just in the shadows out of sight.

How many doors leading to other worlds are out there?

And what do we do if someone like the Silver Witch steps through, into our world?

What if they're already here?

Or someone else much worse?

Black Ooze

There wasn't a crack in the glass or any other indication of damage to the Class 12 Containment Vessel, but the black ooze had gotten out nonetheless. The viscous liquid dripped slowly down to the floor where a puddle had formed. Large bubbles bloomed and popped on the surface of it, letting out puffs of acrid-smelling yellow smoke.

"Do we wake up Rezin or not?"

"We clean it up ourselves, that's what we do."

"But…"

"Nah. No buts. This ain't nothing. Just a little oil spill. We ain't wakin' up Rezin for an oil spill. We get the foamy stuff, we clean it up ourselves."

"This ain't no oil, though, Braggz. This is some damn alien shit. Whiskey said when we loaded up that it was something the bosses back home wanted to look at. Something pseudo-bio-log-ee-coal."

"Right. Pseudo. See, you said it yourself. Pseudo means 'ain't quite.' Meaning this ain't quite alive. It's just oil, Jammerz, pseudo-oil if you wanna get scientific about it. Now calm yourself down and get the foamy stuff. Come on, now. Quit gawkin' at me and go! Why you got that look in your eye all of a sudden like there ain't nobody home?"

"Home…"

"Look at that. You got it on your shoe, now, because you wasn't payin' attention. Forget it. I'll get the damn foamy stuff myself. Just, stand back, will ya? Stand over there. Good. Just wait there and I'll be right back. You're losin' it man. I'm telling you, I do everything 'round this place. If it wasn't for me this ship would fall to pieces."

*

Rezin woke up to the sound of an alarm screeching through his earplugs. He hit the "Silence" button on his comms unit without really analyzing the words flashing in the bright-red dialogue box on his AR display. Braggz and Jammerz would deal with it, whatever it was. That's what maintenance guys were for, after all.

He hated the earplugs, they made his ears hurt and they never fit quite right, but it was all he could do to block out the sounds of the constant overhead chimes and occasional alarms that would wake him from the dead of sleep.

The old ship was falling apart. Everyone knew it but the cheap bastards back home would do nothing to fix it. Too much money. So they were left driving a scrapheap that could barely make it to a platinum-rich asteroid and back without some sort of urgent repair being needed upon return.

A stitch in time saves nine, his father had always said. An old expression passed down for centuries. He guessed that the hotshots back at corporate had never heard it before. They were intent on fixing only what was critically broken, spending no money whatsoever on upkeep or sensible upgrades to the vessel.

If it was his ship he'd do what was right.

He overheard they wanted eight million to overhaul the hyper-drive, and that was just for starters. The whole interior of the freighter was built for utility, not comfort. He understood that. Not having decent furniture or beds, that was one thing. But nothing worked properly anymore. Not even the important stuff, like the electrolysis machine that created their H2O. They'd once had to drink their own piss for the tail end of a trip back because the thing had completely broken down. The rest of the time they were rationing so it didn't overheat.

He threw on a shirt and a pair of pants and went out towards the common room. It wasn't time for morning rations yet, but that was one of the benefits of being on the skeleton crew while everyone else was asleep. You could fudge the rules. And you could take double helpings and nobody said anything because they were all in REM.

"Early breakfast again?" Zeta asked, coming down the hallway grinning.

"And I suppose you're just going this way for a drink of H2O?"

"As long as there's some coffee brewed into that H2O, and a bit of cream to boot. Eggs would be nice too. And bacon."

"Ha. Look who has jokes now. When we get home and we get paid, I'll take you out for all the bacon and eggs you want, how about that?"

"Rezin, are you asking me out?"

"You wish, weirdo. I'm just being a good boss, trying to motivate my subordinates, that's all."

"Wow. You will *never* let me forget the fact that you beat me out for watch commander will you? Are you honestly enjoying the extra twelve credits per cycle that much? Considering all the extra responsibility I'm kinda glad I didn't get the job."

"Droids and maintenance guys take care of everything, Zeta, there is no added responsibility. Just those sweet, sweet credits to look forward to. And bacon and eggs of course. What the hell is this now? Braggz, don't tell me there's another spill down in the accelerator chamber. Please, just, anything but that.”

Braggz was coming out of the clean storage section with a large canister of FOaOMS.

“It ain’t that, boss. Just a little whoopsie over in storage. Gonna get it squared away right now. Jammerz is over there keepin’ an eye on things, making sure all is hunky dory.”

“Great. Just let me know when you’ve got it… Wait. What kind of whoopsie are we talking about anyways? The kind that I need to fill out an incident report for? Because I don’t like that kind of whoopsie.”

“I’ll take care of it. Didn’t I say I was gonna take care of it?”

“Call me when it’s done. And you’re gonna fill me in on the details so we don’t keep having these little slip-ups, okay? There’s too many holes on this ship and we’re starting to take on water.”

“No water in space, boss.”

“Figure of speech, Braggz.”

“Right.”

*

Jammerz wasn’t there when Braggz got back to the storage bay.

“That damn idiot. I tell him to stay put and what does he do? Probably wanders off trailing this shit everywhere on his boot like a dog turd and leaves me to clean up the mess afterwards. Well, I don’t care. This is the last straw. That son of a bitch is gonna get a punch in the tit when I see him next," Braggz was muttering to himself.

He walked over to the spreading puddle of black ooze with the canister of Class 8 Foaming Oil and Organism Management Spray (C-8 FOaOMS) and used it to create a barrier around the stuff. The puddle of black ooze had already spread well past where it was previously. At least there was still a path to walk around it to get to the door at the other end of the corridor, though. If not for that, the mess would look even worse.

He sprayed the foam all over the Class 12 Containment Vessel next, thinking he could use it to keep the ooze more securely within the heavy-duty container.

Just as the large FOaOMs container was nearly running dry, the alarm chime ceased on his Comms Device. Everything was blessedly silent once again. He let his finger relax from the trigger of the spray canister and inspected his work. It looked good to him. The foam was drying and creating a hard coating that would keep everything in check until they got back to earth. Then it would be the offload guys' problem.

A nearby hatch opened and a small spherical droid flew over. It hovered in front of the foam-covered mess and began to emit a criss-crossing series of lasers which inspected his handiwork. After a few moments of deliberation, it chimed approvingly and a green smiley face appeared on the face of the droid. Then it zoomed off to attend to other matters.

"Finally."

He dropped the FOaOMs container to the ground and left it there, in case the spill needed a top-up later on, and went walking back the way he had come.

"Breakfast time."

*

Rezin was sitting at the table in the common room with Zeta, eating their bowls of carbos, when Braggz sauntered in, his chin up and shoulders back like he had just accomplished some grand feat.

He grabbed a pouch from the fridge and came over to sit with them at the only table in the place, setting his bottle of H_2O down with a loud clang.

"Fix the problem?"

"It ain't chimin' no more, is it?"

Rezin let out a sigh. Why was it always so hard to get answers around here? His attempts at common-sense questioning with maintenance personnel, Braggz in particular, were always met with vagueness and low-key hostility.

"So are you gonna make me play twenty questions or are you gonna tell me why I got woken up by a level four breach?"

"It was nothing a little foamy stuff couldn't fix. Just some oil, that's all."

"What the hell are you talking about, Braggz? There's no oil in Storage B."

"You know, that black stuff in the heavy-duty containment vessel that Whiskey was so excited about."

They both dropped their spoons on the table, their jaws hanging open.

"It… Got out?"

*

"See? The foamy stuff kept it all tidy and now it ain't spreadin' around no more."

He had to admit, there was no sign of a leak anywhere. His heart was still pounding out of his chest, though.

"What about this?" Zeta asked from the other side of the mess. "It's a shoe print."

Braggz looked a little bit embarrassed for a few seconds before admitting, "Oh, right. Well, I guess Jammerz did kind of step in it. I told him to wait here but the idiot wandered off."

"He… stepped into the puddle?"

"Yeah."

Rezin's stomach suddenly had a lead weight inside of it, for reasons he could not discern. The whole situation was rubbing him the wrong way. The fact that they didn't truly know what the ooze was didn't make things any easier, and certainly did nothing to reassure him.

Not good. Something tells me this is very much not a good thing.

"Zeta, go hail base, will ya? See if they've got any insights into this stuff that we don't, based on Whiskey's assessment."

He debated waking up Captain Grippe, but decided against it. His mind's eye saw the cold steely gaze of his looking back at his own, asking a million questions, asking how he could let such a thing happen. He wanted to delay that as long as possible, maybe indefinitely if he could manage to cover up these idiots' mistakes.

Zeta hurried off in the direction of the Comm Center.

"Braggz, this is really important. Where the hell did Jammerz go?"

*

Rezin was following the footprints. He had given Braggz a tongue lashing for a while, then sent him as far away as possible. He told him to go search the ship and find his missing colleague. What that moron could possibly be thinking he had no idea.

Rezin was beating himself up too, though. He had slept through too many alarms. Become too complacent.

I'm going to start trying again, he thought to himself. *I can't afford to lose this job. Just let everything be okay so I don't lose this job. Please.*

He sprayed the foamy stuff down on each shoe print as he walked past, but the canister was almost empty. Pretty soon he would have to go back and get a fresh bottle. Assuming there even was a fresh bottle.

"Rezin, come in. REZIN!"

Zeta was talking to him through the Comms device but her voice sounded like it was coming from underwater. Barely a word of it could be made out. He spoke back to her calmly. No sense losing your shit now. You're the leader, act like it.

"Go ahead, Zeta."

"The sat-comm is malfunctioning. There's all kinds of noise. I can't get anybody back at base."

"Keep trying. If you don't get a response in the next five minutes, meet me over in cryo - I'm headed that direction."

He kept walking along, spraying the FOaOMS every time he came across a shoe print. They were becoming faded and more difficult to see in the dim, flickering lights of the corridor.

It was about time to check up on Braggz. No telling what that man would do if left to his own devices.

"Braggz, come in. Come in, Braggz."

Nothing.

"Do you hear me talking, you big dumb idiot?" He winced self-consciously after saying that. *Great job, Mr. Watch Commander, way to motivate your subordinates. Where did you learn your leadership skills, anyways?*

A few more seconds of silence, and then Braggz's voice came over the Comms device.

"You're gonna want to see this, boss."

*

Once he reached the cryo-chambers Braggz was gone. Everyone else had vanished too.

Each chamber tank was empty with no sign of the crew members who should have occupied them. Missing lights meant that the room was dark and it was difficult to see in the confined space. At least there were very few places to hide.

"Where the hell is everybody?" Zeta asked, coming in just behind him.

He nearly jumped out of his skin at the sound of her, startled despite his training telling him to stay calm. He fought to speak as plainly as possible, and it came out cracking, making him sound like a teenage boy.

"Not sure. They should still be in phase two. This makes no sense."

"It's like somebody just aborted the process midway through. But why would anybody do that? And who?"

"Jammerz, I guess…"

"But why the hell would he do that, Rezin?"

"I don't have the faintest idea, Zeta."

She took a deep breath and let it out, looking down at her own trembling hands as if willing them to settle.

"So what now, Watch Commander?"

*

Zeta raced down the echoing corridor towards the bridge as fast as her feet could carry her. She thought it was wise considering the circumstances for them to stick together, *but men always believe they know better, even when they're wrong.* Rezin was a good man and a passable leader, but no different in that regard.

He had told her to secure the bridge while he went to the weapons bay for supplies. The fact that the cryo-stasis had been aborted meant serious bodily harm was possible to the crew members affected. Jammerz knew that and he had aborted anyways - he was the only one of the four of them who could have done it. And logic followed that if he had done that, he was not altogether in his right mind.

The ooze from the containment vessel was potentially having some sort of effect on Jammerz that was making him lose his best judgement (which wasn't all that grand to begin with) -

and someone like that could not be allowed to enter the bridge with its sensitive equipment. They would need to locate him ASAP and secure him in lock-up.

Suddenly, the lights in the hallway flickered and went out.

Zeta waited for the back-up power to come on. It usually only took a second. But instead the lights stayed dead. The darkness was total, suffocating in its utter blackness. She couldn't see an inch in front of her face when she lifted her hand in front of her eyes. Suddenly she was acutely aware of how precarious their situation was, floating through space on this barely functioning barge.

If the lights were out, did that mean the navigational systems were out too? The engine? No, she realized she could still feel the thrum of the warp drive system radiating beneath her feet from the center of the ship. Hopefully it was just the lights, after all.

Gradually the after image of the hallway disappeared from her vision and she was left swimming in darkness as black as the bottom of the ocean, or the depths of space between stars.

"Rezin, can you hear me?" she said hesitantly into the comms device.

There was no response.

A soft clicking sound went quickly past her instead, then was gone in an instant. She jumped, unsure what it could have been. The ship's equipment sometimes made strange noises, but she had never heard anything like that.

"Braggz? Jammerz? Rezin? Anybody???"

Again, there was no answer from her comms.

She remembered suddenly that the device on her wrist had an emergency light built into it. Reaching up her hand, she struggled to find the hidden button.

Click, click, clack, click, clack, click, click

Something sped past her again, this time closer to the ceiling, moving in the opposite direction.

Finally, she found the button and a dim light was emitted from the comms device on her wrist. Shining it forwards, she began to walk again, taking a deep, shuddering breath as she did so. Her legs felt like gelatin.

Zeta's eyes scanned the ceiling and the floors for the source of the noise, but found nothing. She was alone once again.

*

Weapons Bay was a mess. Attempting to find a fully charged thermal core was proving exceedingly difficult and Rezin kept coming up with half-charged ones. He settled on the one that appeared the most reliable and slotted it into a rifle. He grabbed a pistol from the charging rack next and a few photon grenades.

Everything he found he threw into a duffel bag, except for the rifle which he kept loaded and with the safety off, slung over his shoulder, ready to fire. Carefully, he set the duffel bag down next to him to free up his hands while he finished what he had to do.

He would give Zeta the pistol once he reached the bridge. It had been a risk sending her alone, with Jammerz running around not in his right mind, but he needed privacy for what he was about to do next.

He pushed aside a large crate to expose a well-hidden secret panel. Lifting the corner of it back, it revealed a hole. Rezin reached his arm inside the wall and groped around, until he managed to find the pouch. With an effort, he pulled it out, feeling the weight of it in his hand.

The chunk of platinum was heavy and would fetch a good price on the black market. But if they had to jump on an escape pod and blow up the ship in a hurry it would be lost. His instincts told him to take it now, while he still could.

After unzipping the duffel bag he put the pouch inside and then closed it up again.

"What you got there, boss?"

The voice behind him sent shivers down his spine. It was flat and emotionless. Despite a question having been asked there was no hint of curiosity in it.

He turned around and saw Jammerz standing behind him, blocking the doorway. His eyes were black as polished opals and his mouth twitched, waiting for an answer. There looked to be something moving inside, pushing against his cheeks and deforming them like a huge hunk of bubblegum.

"Jammerz. You spooked me, man. Glad you're okay," he said, realizing as he spoke the words that they were not true. Jammerz was not okay. Nothing was okay now nor would it ever be again.

"I asked you a question. What you got there? WHAT YOU GOT THERE? WHAT YOU GOT THERE!? WHAT YOU GOT THERE!?? BOSSSSMAN!!!???"

The crewman began to stalk towards him, repeating the question over and over and over again, his voice sped-up and high-pitched, a clicking noise overlaid below it. Black veins pulsed at his temples, his eyes reddened with burst blood vessels on both sides.

Then suddenly he began to choke and gag as something emerged from his mouth, pushing past his tongue and grabbing the corners of his mouth with thin, long, insectile legs, it pulled itself out, past his teeth and lips. Its antenna twitched as if sniffing the air.

Something like a cockroach, but much bigger, came out of his mouth. Its head came next, followed by a thorax and legs, large, spindly legs that were dreadful and black. More were following after it. The massive bug crawled across his face, down Jammerz' body and was soon on the floor, racing towards Rezin, legs clicking audibly across the hard tiles, and he forgot all about his rifle and the bag of weapons laying at his feet. There were more of the huge bugs on the ceiling, he noticed, and crawling under the door and moving towards him from the corridor.

He felt heavy insectile legs, covered with fine hairs, touch him, and the thing crawled up his boot and into his pant leg, those horrifying, disgusting legs sticking to his skin as it moved upwards, towards his crotch. The hairs of it brushed against him and he felt an overwhelming rush of revulsion, gagging and nearly vomiting as it reached his belt and continued up his chest.

Wherever it touched him, he felt numb afterwards, he noticed. As if that flesh was dead and gone.

The lights in the room suddenly flickered and went out. The last thing Rezin saw was Jammerz standing in front of him, smiling wide as more bugs poured out from his mouth, small and large in size. He was coughing, choking, and laughing as they marched out in droves and raced toward him. Huge, mutant cockroaches crawling out from between his cracked, dark purple lips.

*

Long before Zeta reached the bridge, she realized there was something wrong. The clicking sounds had been everywhere and she finally managed to spot one of the creatures making the noises.

Massive cockroaches. That's what they looked like, anyways. And their numbers were growing larger by the second. She could tell by the increased presence of them that they were capable of multiplying rapidly. It would only be a short period of time before the ship was overrun.

She rounded the corner and stopped in her tracks, gasping for air that would no longer reach her lungs. Legs buckling, she dropped to her knees and stared at what had become of the ship's bridge. The sacred thing she had aspired to command one day, now lost.

At least the mystery of the missing crew members had been solved. They were hanging upside down, encased in cocoon-like tombs made of slick black webbing. Only their faces were visible, their eyes covered but their mouths and noses covered with organic tubing, leading up towards the ceiling. There, a huge sack was suspended, inflating and deflating chambers interlaced with veins made it look like a massive heart slowly beating.

Black ooze was seeping out from structures connected to it which were all across the floor. They looked like giant roots, weeping poison which dpread across the ground like an oil spill.

With her sharp eyes, Zeta saw what was happening. The skin of the crewmembers writhed and things could be seen crawling and moving beneath the surface. They were food to these creatures, nothing more. They were being consumed from the inside out.

She had seen enough. Spinning on her heel, she fled from the room just as a strange sound like an egg cracking began to be heard. She had no desire to stick around and find out what it meant.

Zeta had only one destination in mind - to get to weapons bay and find Rezin. She hoped it wasn't already too late. The whole ship was already infested by those *things*.

Jammerz had only gotten a little bit on his shoe. What would happen if the ship docked back on earth and was unloaded?

She shuddered to think of the possibilities.

They had to stop the ship from making it back. The alternative was too risky.

The ship was massive, and the weapons bay was far from the bridge, but she eventually arrived there, beginning to hear the sounds of footsteps racing after her far back in the distance, down the corridor.

Entering weapons bay, she found that Rezin was already gone. So was every single piece of weaponry. Every gun and grenade, every piece of armor, everything had vanished.

The footsteps were getting closer, she realized, moving steadily towards her. They would arrive at any second.

Terrified, she pulled off one of the air-vent covers nearby and went inside, closing it up behind her. The air was hot and thick inside, full of dust which tickled her nose.

She went forward on her hands and knees in the tight, confined space, unsure of where she was going or what she was going to do. All she knew was that the vents connected everything and this one would take her someplace else. Maybe to the room with the escape pods. That option was beginning to look like it made the most sense.

The sound of someone entering the weapons bay could be heard from behind her and she dared not move while they were speaking.

"I know I saw her come in here. She's gone." Soft clicking noises could be heard beneath the distorted voice. It sounded like Jammerz, but who he was talking to she couldn't say.

She crept forward on her hands and knees as quietly as she could, desperate to get away from him. Where she was going, she still did not know.

As she struggled forward in the small space, her heart began to jack-hammer faster and faster. The darkness was total, and if something were to sneak up from behind and attack her, she would be unable to turn around and fight back.

This thought plagued her with worry and she found herself hearing things and wondering what the noises meant in the darkness. Someone behind her? Up ahead around the next corner? Who could say?

A clicking, tapping noise came from somewhere far off, echoing through the blackness. It was a noise that was becoming all too familiar.

Suddenly someone grabbed her leg. An ice-cold hand reached from the darkness behind her and she thought she would die of a heart-attack in that instant. Her voice caught in her throat or she would have screamed as well, but instead she made a choked whimpering sound and said a few unrecognizable words that might have resembled a plea for mercy, or a very quick death.

"I ain't gonna kill ya," said a voice from behind her. "Even though I should. The way you guys left me alone like that. I almost got murdered, y'know."

"Braggz!?"

"Well it ain't your Aunt Betty," he was wheezing and had to catch his breath after speaking this last sentence.

"Are you okay?"

"Yeah, I think so. Man, I really gotta quit vapin'. Come on, let's get moving. Where are we going, anyhow? I've just been hidin' in here waitin' to die, more or less."

"We're getting off this damn ship," Zeta said. An idea was beginning to take shape in her mind. "But we need to make a stop first."

*

"Are you sure about this? The bosses back home are gonna be pissed."

"The bosses back home aren't the ones fighting off roaches the size of chihuahuas. We have no choice. It's either this or by the time we get back to Earth on the escape pods it'll be overrun."

Braggz didn't look entirely convinced, but he took the chain from around his neck and inserted the key into the slot. Zeta did the same and they turned them clockwise at the same time, towards the setting marked, *Engage*.

The proverbial big red button was just in front of them and Zeta lifted the glass cover up and took a deep breath.

Then, without another word, she slammed her fist down hard on it. Nothing happened.

"You gotta be kidding me."

She smashed it with her fist again. And again. Then a dozen more times in rapid succession.

Finally, an alarm blared to life and a voice began to speak over the P.A. - sounding bored and robotic.

"ALERT! ALERT! Self-destruct protocols have been activated. Please proceed to the nearest escape pod in bays one through four. This is not a drill. Alert. Alert. Self-destruct protocols have been activated..." It repeated the message several more times as whooping alarms rang out in every area of the ship. Red lights were now flashing in lazy arcs as well, illuminating the ceiling in their glow.

Maintenance droids emerged from holes in the walls and began zooming around the ship in every direction, carrying out their new missions as the ship was now destined for oblivion.

"Okay," said Zeta. "*Now* we can get the hell outta here." Of course Braggz was already climbing into the air vent, crawling away.

She suddenly felt something crawling up her leg, which went ice cold and would not move once it had gone past. It tickled its way up her spine and her knees buckled as it went up her neck, into her ear, and made a home inside her skull.

This is not good. This is very much not a good thing, Zeta had time to think, before a piercing headache consumed her mind and a ringing noise like tinnitus.

After that, all was black.

*

Braggz was watching the freighter get smaller in the distance from the safety of his escape pod.

It was too bad Zeta hadn't made it. She was one of the good ones. Without her, the creatures would have gotten back to Earth and taken over. After all, it took two people to activate the self-destruct mechanism and he wouldn't have had the guts to do it without her, anyways.

He said a silent thank you to her for her sacrifice. They'd throw a parade for her back home, after he told them about what she'd done. Mankind was no match for those Herculean roaches. The standard ones were bad enough.

The freighter exploded silently in the distance, the white light of the blast burning his retinas.

"Told 'em that ship would fall to pieces without me," he muttered to himself, setting the positioning system controls to target home base. Earth.

Once it was all programmed in, he just had to sit back, relax, and wait for the slow journey to be over.

The escape pod began to pick up speed and the stars became a blur as he raced towards his home world. Braggz closed his eyes and tried to sleep, but he couldn't. There was a noise keeping him awake, coming from near his feet.

"What the hell is that?"

Click,   click,   clack,   click,   clack,   click,   click

New Colour I Invented will Kill Lots of People

All the trouble I've caused, the pain, the death... It all started with a breakthrough.

I'm an artist and painter by trade, but also an inventor. I like to spend some of my spare time experimenting by creating new colours. It's a hobby but I also make some money on the side, primarily through a shade of purple I made that is marginally popular as well as an ultra dark shade of black. That one is fun because it looks really weird in everyday life to see a coffee mug or a t-shirt that is unnaturally colourless. Like a black hole or something.

But this new one is different. I call it grurple.

The name is dumb, I know. But it's got my last name buried in it, and it's a combination of the words green and purple. That makes sense because that's what the colour is...

Except that doesn't describe it well enough. Because people have combined those two colours before and it just turns into an ugly brownish black barf sort of hue that nobody would want to use for anything.

But this is different. It retains the essence of purple and green and makes something never before seen and amazing with them in the process. It's like looking at a rainbow for the first time – startling and otherworldly.

But since I created it, I've been seeing things. And they're all the same colour: grurple.

My laptop, for instance. I turned it off because the colours had begun to look strange, and the problem had proved to be uncorrectable. That was when I saw movement in the corner of the blank screen, the reflection of something sliding just out of view at the edge. I looked over my shoulder and saw there was nothing there.

I left my room and went to the bathroom to splash cold water on my face. The computer could be fixed, I thought to myself. I'd just take it over to my friend Dave's place, since he always knew what to do with computer problems.

In the reflection of the bathroom mirror I saw the tub was no longer the old-fashioned shade of horrible out-of-fashion pink that it had been before, the one it had always been since I moved in. It was now grurple.

It was as if someone had come into my home and replaced my bathtub with someone else's. But of course that was impossible. My hands started to tremble, my heartbeat quickening as it felt like the world began to turn sideways on its axis.

I tried to calm myself down, focusing on my breathing, focusing on anything that wasn't the bathtub.

The bathroom mirror was dirty so I decided to quickly clean it to distract myself. As I finished wiping it off, I saw something in the corner of the glass surface, slipping out of view just as my eye noticed it, just like earlier in the computer monitor's reflection. The slender, pointed tail of a lizard? That was how it looked anyways.

I went out into the hallway to check if a stray Komodo dragon had snuck into my house somehow, but again there was nothing. I couldn't help but think that the colour of whatever it was looked familiar, though – whatever it was, it was coloured grurple.

I got the impression of something looming and large, crafty and elusive, its skin rough and thick like that of a dinosaur.

Suddenly it was there again, at the periphery of my vision, but upon inspection I saw only empty space. Nearby I could sense something enormous and awful, like a storm head rolling in.

Deciding to get out of the house, I left with my laptop to walk over to Dave's place. He was only a few blocks over.

It was a sunny day outside, humid and clear. I immediately wished I had brought my sunglasses but decided not to go back for them. It was a short walk.

As I ambled down the street, lugging my heavy old laptop, I started to have more and more trouble seeing. The sun was so bright I found myself blinking repeatedly, then having more and more difficulty opening my eyes each time. My vision became reduced to momentary glimpses between each blink until my eyes simply forced themselves closed and I couldn't see at all anymore. The only thing I could see was the new colour I had created, it filled my vision instead of the usual darkness when I blinked.

I didn't know where I was, only that I had been walking on the sidewalk a moment before. There was no shade nearby and I was stranded, completely blind in the middle of my walk. Unfortunately for me I had unwittingly crossed into the roadway and was no longer on the sidewalk but standing in the middle of a busy intersection.

Suddenly someone tackled me, landing on me and sending me flying. I heard a car's tires squealing and smelled burnt brake pads, a loud bang and the crunching of metal and breaking of glass.

Then people were yelling at me.

"WHAT THE HELL WERE YOU DOING STANDING IN THE ROAD LIKE THAT!? YOU SHOULD BE DEAD!" came the chorus from the people all around.

I was in the ditch and my vision came back suddenly and I had no trouble seeing as fear and adrenaline took over my body.

Two cars were mangled and wrapped up together in the roadway where they had crashed into each other. The drivers were both bloodied and unconscious in their seats and people were pulling them out as a fire started to spread from the engine of one vehicle.

"I couldn't see! I couldn't see!" I screamed, but nobody listened.

The police came and took a statement from me, then gave me a tongue-lashing I would never forget. I told them it was sun-blindness (which was true, I suppose) and they let me off without a charge of public endangerment causing bodily harm.

Thankfully everyone survived and nobody had any lasting effects from the accident. If it hadn't been for the stranger who pushed me out of the way I would have been dead. But he wasn't too impressed with my behaviour, either.

My laptop was a write-off and I limped home with a quickly-swelling twisted ankle.

When I got back there I could sense it waiting for me. It was like I could hear its breathing. The creature I had brought forth with my invention.

I decided I needed to destroy it. There was something wrong with that colour. It wasn't meant for this world - I could tell that already.

The experimental batches of grurple were in my studio, in the basement, and I rushed down there.

The hairs on the back of my neck stood up as I felt the thing following behind me. I was too afraid to look back.

As I raced down the stairs I nearly tripped, my bad ankle giving out on me as I hobbled down the wooden steps. My studio was just ahead and I raced inside and went to my locked cabinet where I stored all my experimental work.

The paintings I had done in the new colour were there, as well as the jars containing the hue itself. It was a shame to destroy it, but it had to be done. It wasn't supposed to be here. I should never have brought it into existence.

Pouring paint down the drain is a really bad idea but I was desperate so I went over to the sink with the small test batch and opened it, tilting the container to dump it out. But then something, a voice, stopped me and my skin went ice cold, goosebumps spreading across it.

"How did you divine my colours?" hissed the thing from behind me. From the shadows.

It wasn't real. The monster wasn't real. I just had to pour out the paint.

But something was stopping me.

My eyes were drawn to the test paintings I had done. One of them stood out among the rest and I found myself setting down the jar of paint and looking at it.

I couldn't remember painting it.

The image showed a beast coloured vividly in grurple. It shone and reflected the light back at me, making me think of things. Awful things. Beautiful things. I couldn't tell the difference between them after a while as they flashed before my eyes.

A dead girl at the bottom of a well

Roses in bloom

Roadkill with maggots

Bloated corpse coming in with the tide

Rotten skin being peeled from a hand like a banana

Lemon meringue pie

A sunset over the ocean

Broken fingernails on the inside of a coffin lid

"How did you manage to paint me? Did you see me in a vision? For when you made this I had not yet been to see you. You summoned me, in a way. With this."

A long talon on an even longer finger reached out and pointed at the image I had made. The one I had forgotten making.

I could feel the thing behind me, its breathing hot on my neck.

"Over the years I have been named many things. They have called me Charon, Azrael, Shiva, and Anubis. I have NEVER seen a depiction as striking as this, though. You perfectly captured my… essence."

"Thank you," I croaked.

"Why don't you do more of these? It would be a shame to waste such a precious talent as yours."

My hand hesitated and I found myself not wanting to destroy the paint after all. I wanted to use it. There was an image I had always wanted to depict and the paint would be perfect for it, I just knew it.

I set up my easel and began to draw, then prime, and then laid down the big blocks of colour for what would be my greatest work to date.

The piece consumed my life for three days. For 72 hours I did nothing but paint.

Once it was complete, I knew it was the best thing I had ever made.

The image depicted Charon, the ferryman from Greek mythology. He was taking someone across the river Styx from our world into the underworld, the afterlife. The Ferryman himself was richly painted in my new colour.

"You should share it with the world," said the voice again.

And I found myself wanting to do as he suggested. So I did.

I took it to galleries and the first few people who saw it didn't really like it as much as I did. Despite an excellent composition the consensus among them was that the colour of Charon was off – that the colour of him just looked like a brownish-black barf sort of hue. They didn't see the new colour for some reason.

So I brought it to more galleries, circling out further and further from my home, until one owner I showed it to saw it and I knew he REALLY saw it.

The well-dressed man immediately exclaimed in delight and took it from my hands, holding the piece up to inspect it. Fawning over it, he told me how much he loved the painting and insisted on buying it for himself. He looked mesmerized and couldn't take his eyes from the piece.

"I'll pay any price," he said, reaching for his checkbook.

I wanted to work with him more so I gave him a reasonable price and told him I would be back. I would have plenty more paintings to share with him. All with similar subject matter.

The thought had occurred to me that I needed to do a series of paintings focusing on Charon. But that would require a lot more paint.

A couple more gallons would suffice, I told myself. So I ordered my supplies and within a week I had another large batch of grurple made up.

My next paintings were similar to the first. I rarely slept or ate anymore, I just worked in my studio non-stop. The pounds were shedding from me and I needed to make new notches on my belt pretty soon just to keep my pants up.

The only thing that seemed important was painting.

Until I called the gallery and heard the news.

It turned out the owner of the place who had bought my painting of Charon was dead. He had committed suicide. He had stopped leaving his house, becoming more and more isolated and catatonic, doing nothing but staring at the painting. Until one day he had slit his wrists in front of it. He positioned furniture to lean against so that he could die while sitting up, admiring it.

Green and purple, purple and green. Life and death, death and life.

I thought about this more and more after that. It's hard to want to paint when you know that your work will kill someone. Maybe not everyone, but those who can truly see what lies beneath the colours, what glimmers back in the reflections.

Do *you* want to see a sample of my work?

The Real Count Chocula

This is probably going to come as a shock to most of you, but here goes...

Count Chocula is a real person. Actually, a real vampire, if you want to get specific about it. We met in the seventies. I was his advertising campaign manager.

Unlike most vampires who stayed in Transylvania due to monarchistic duties, he chose to reside in Belgium where better chocolate could be found, although he visited France and Germany frequently as well. He was a connoisseur of the stuff - chocolate, that is. But he also enjoyed a glass of blood with dinner, and a nightcap at bedtime. For the anti-oxidants, he told me once.

It was on one of those frequent trips to France that he met a representative from a cereal company looking for a new mascot. General Mills.

There's nothing quite like working with a vampire, and Count Chocula was no exception. I met him at the General Mills head office where the head marketing manager was holding a meeting. I came in as an outside consultant, but I was soon hired on full time.

"Mr. James, I want you to meet our newest asset. This is Count Chocula the fourth," Mr. Scotson said, gesturing to a man in brown and purple robes. It was the seventies so of course he had massive sideburns and what would be considered today to be a ridiculous up-do - split right down the middle like Shemp and then drawn upward into spikes which looked like brown horns made of hair.

I shook hands with the tall, strange-looking man. He had two very large, sharpened buck teeth which gleamed white in the bright light of the conference room.

"I love vhat you did vith the Frosted Corn Flakes campaign," said The Count. "That tiger gets me everytime! Ah, ah, ah!"

His belly laugh sounded very vampiric. But other than that he looked like your friendly, run of the mill mascot. Not the cartoon, of course, that creation was simply styled after his look.

"So here's what we were thinking, James," Mr. Scotson said, pointing to a presentation board. "Count Chocula cereal - they're CHOCK full of cinnamon!"

He looked excited and paused for my response. Count Chocula waited with a big smile on his face for my approval.

"Nobody is doing cinnamon! Nobody! We'd be the first ones with a cinnamon-based cereal! Big clumps of it that are crunchy at first but they dissolve in the milk and get deliciously soggy! What do you think, Mr. James? Is that a winner or what?"

I tried not to burst the man's bubble too brutally but the idea stank. It was right there in front of them, how could they not see it?

"Tell him the catch-phrase," someone said from across the table, sensing my reticence.

"I vant to cinnamon your blood!" The Count said enthusiastically. Everyone grinned wide and looked at me with expectant eyes.

"Did you guys ever consider... Count Chocula being made with... chocolate?"

Everyone's jaws dropped. Spontaneous applause broke out and I was lifted up on several people's shoulders as they sang songs of my great idea, carrying me on a chair around the office, being careful not to be too specific in the lyrics of their impromptu celebratory songs, since spies from Kellogg's could be anywhere... There were suspected moles in the office.

"Brilliant idea, Mr. James," said Count Chocula afterwards, clapping me on the back. "I vant this man in charge of all advertising for my brand. He's my guy, understand, Scotson?"

The old manager grudgingly agreed (I didn't come cheap, after all) and the three of us shook on the deal.

It was the beginning of a strange partnership and an even stranger friendship.

The start of the seventies was upon us and we began things off with a bang. Regulations were loose back then, and it showed in the ingredients. Or, rather, it didn't show. FrankenBerry's run in with the law for using a banned indigestible pigment resulting in "FrankenBerry Stool" (pink-coloured poop for the lay-person) wouldn't happen for a few more years and we were all living the good life. Riding high on a wave of profits. The FDA had bigger fish to fry, at least for the time being.

As sales of our sugar and cocoa-laden cereal began to skyrocket, I was touted as a king of the cereal advertising industry. Our chocolate cereal idea was the envy of every other brand. The Count was happy to stay hidden in the shadows and collect his cash, people believing he was just what we claimed he was, a loveable cartoon mascot. Nobody knew the darkest truths yet, not even me.

We were doing great at the beginning - with wealth and power that few people could dream of. I used to keep boxes of cash in my closets, in my cupboards, all over my house. I didn't trust the banks. I still don't - not after what they did to George Jung.

We had women, cars, yachts, bling, you name it. We'd hit a chocolate goldmine. Kids weren't used to that level of sugar in their cereals back in those days. In order to get even close to the taste they wanted, kids had to heap it on themselves by the tablespoon, and parents didn't like to look at that. Not one bit. Not with the price of sugar as high as it was...

But what they didn't see didn't hurt them. A market was out there sitting wide open for a cheap, sweet, somewhat digestible breakfast cereal. So we pumped those toasted oats full of sugar, fat, dye, and cocoa powder, and set them loose on society.

With all that money came power and freedoms we never could have imagined. All of us pretended not to know what The Count did with his share of the cash. But sooner or later we all knew. We all found out one by one, in our own ways.

I discovered the truth when he invited me to his castle in Belgium one summer. It was 73, I think, and we were riding high still, with nothing but hope and big plans for the future on the horizon. But I didn't realize The Count had different aspirations. Darker and much grander plans than simply cereal production.

His castle was located on a mountainous pass and was very difficult to reach. I rented a car and it barely made it up the steep slopes. Everyone in town seemed terrified when I told them where I was headed and said to be careful. They said there were rumors of a great monster that lived in the mountains. A huge, winged beast.

A storm was brewing when I arrived, a black cloud coming in over the mountains to my right as I pulled up to the giant castle.

I hurried quickly up the front steps, feeling as if there were eyes upon me, watching me from above.

There was a large brass knocker on the huge wooden doors at the front of the house, wrought iron and shaped in the face of a sharp-toothed bat. I used it to knock and the door swung open by itself.

"Count?" I called out, walking into the dusty castle foyer. There seemed to be nobody home. And yet I still couldn't help but feel as if I was being watched.

"Ah, Mr. James. A pleasure to see you here."

The Count was suddenly behind me, although I hadn't seen him on the stairs outside. All I'd heard was a flap and flutter behind me like a giant pair of wings.

"You surprised me! Good to see you, Count. How have you been?"

"Excellent. I've finally gotten everything I've ever wanted… All thanks to you."

He closed the door behind him and I realized I was cornered. His face no longer looked friendly. In fact, he looked quite upset.

"Is everything okay, Count? You don't look like yourself…"

He dropped his cape to the stone floor and unfurled a set of massive bat wings. They were ragged and torn, sewn together with scraps of flesh. I saw the remnants of human bodies sewn together with crude stitches - faces mid-scream, there were nipples and stretch lines and all the imperfections of the random unfortunate souls he had chosen to piece together to make his masterpieces - his fully functional bat wings.

"Holy shit, Count... Some people buy a private jet... I guess you took it a step further. How much did you pay for those things?"

I saw blood was dripping down his chin and onto his brown suit.

He didn't answer me.

"Oh no... Have you been blood-binging again? You know how you get when you're like that.... All grabby and bitey... I don't like it when you're like this. Can I go?"

His eyes blazed red with sudden fire.

"You are the one spying for Kellogg's! I got the call this morning from our man over there! He said it's for sure. You're the man on the inside."

My heart began to pound with fear as he stepped towards me. His massive wings blocked out the light and he looked tall and menacing, his sharp buck teeth dripping freshly consumed blood.

"You lie. They said you've been feeding them secrets all year!"

"They're just trying to drive a wedge between us! I came up with the idea of putting the chocolate in Count Chocula, remember? If it wasn't for me you'd be nothing! Cinnamon clumps that get soggy - that was your idea! Nobody wants to eat that! Nobody wants to eat cinnamon cereal!"

I realized I was making things worse and I quickly shut up.

His gaze darkened and he lunged at me like a wild animal, his wings drawn back as he closed the distance between us in an instant.

He grabbed me by the neck and began to choke me, squeezing my trachea between his fingers with so much force I could barely speak for weeks afterwards.

"It wasn't me!" I managed to squeak. "You can't kill me! I made you what you are!"

My hands were in his face, trying to push him away, and he suddenly recoiled, dropping me.

"Blah! Vhat is on your hands!? They taste terrible!!"

"Oh. There was pasta on the plane. Garlic bread too. Lots of garlic in all of it!"

I exhaled a stink bomb of garlic breath in his face and he backed away even further.

I'd also stuck two of the garlic breadsticks in my pocket and I took them out and made an impromptu cross with them.

"Blah! Vhy? Vhy? Don't do this to me Mr. James, we're partners!"

"Not anymore," I said, tossing one of the cold breadsticks at his forehead and burning him badly with it.

He crumpled to the floor and I raced past him and unlocked the door, leaving as quickly as I could.

I got back to my car and drove out of there as fast as possible. A shadow seemed to follow me as I raced down the steep mountain roads, blocking out the light of the moon. A huge bird, it looked like. But I knew it was something much worse.

Without a single stop along the way I made it to the airport and left my rental car just outside the front entrance of the hanger, not caring if it got towed.

I got on the phone with General Mills as soon as I got back stateside.

"I'll never work with that blood-sucking son of a bitch again," I told him. "I'll keep my agreed upon percentages and stay as a silent partner from now on. You guys are on your own with that lunatic."

"We're sorry to lose you," said the general. But he didn't argue. My mind was made up.

He relieved me of my duties and I went on to other jobs and other opportunities. Ten years later a new CEO was in charge and I pitched him an idea that he absolutely loved.

Cinnamon Toast Crunch.

You're welcome.

I Bought a Creepy Painting in an Online Auction

I've always loved creepy shit. It started off with horror books. Reading Goosebumps in elementary school, later graduating on to Stephen King, Shirley Jackson, Mark Z. Danielewski, and a myriad of others.

Eventually I started writing my own scary stuff, mostly because I wanted to create stories that I would want to read for myself as a horror fan. After about a decade, I got to be marginally successful, and nowadays it's how I pay the bills.

I never thought my life would turn into a horror story, though. How ironic is that?

*

Some people decorate their houses with colourful vases stuffed with flowers, Normal Rockwell paintings, knickknacks, and crystal sculptures of dolphins and fairy princesses. I prefer to cover my walls with freaky drawings, paintings, and prints of artworks by Francisco Goya, Anthony Christopher, and Salvadore Dali - the weirder and darker the better. I like my art the same as I like my novels - horrifying and unsettling.

So when my friend Marcus sent me a text with the title: "Check out this painting of a creepy old lady!" I laughed and clicked on the link without too much thought.

I was redirected to an obscure foreign website where old and new paintings were being sold in a never-ending online auction. I hadn't heard of the auction company before, but that didn't stop me from pulling out my credit card as soon as I saw the image that had been shared with me.

A woman's hypnotic and bizarre face stared back at me, looking life-like and yet utterly surrealistic. Not to mention terrifying. Her pupils were too big and too black. Her smile stretched too wide, like a Dr. Zeus' character, but devoid of any kindness or good humor.

It was a portrait of an elderly woman who appeared to be in her seventies or eighties. She was dressed in dark, monastic-looking clothing which I guessed to be a couple hundred years old. I figured it was a reproduction of an older painting - since the price tag was only fifty dollars - the style similar to a renaissance painting, the brush strokes well hidden, her face photographically realistic as if painted by an old world master.

The woman in the painting was sitting on an antique wooden chair with embellishments carved into the posts of the backrest. Her eyes seemed to follow me and looked back at me maliciously.

The impression I got was that she was a real person staring back at me from the portrait, like glancing through a window and seeing the face of an unknown stranger standing just outside. I felt as if she could reach through the screen and grab hold of me if she wanted to.

Without hesitating, I put in my credit card details before somebody else could buy it. The thing was just too weird to pass up.

After a week or so of waiting, the parcel arrived on my doorstep. I had semi-forgotten about it by that point, since I had been busy with other things. But as soon as I saw its distinctive flat, rectangular shape wrapped in brown parcel paper, I remembered my impulse purchase and brought it inside with giddy delight, happy to unwrap it right away.

As soon as I had it open, my heart dropped and I felt sick, like I could throw up.

I had rarely felt buyer's remorse, but I definitely did when I looked down at the woman's face staring back at mine. She looked alive. And she looked undeniably evil. I couldn't explain why I felt that way, but I did.

The idea of hanging the thing on my wall repulsed me. Just touching it felt like picking up a handful of maggots. It made my skin crawl.

After putting it down, I wanted nothing more than to get rid of it. But it felt wrong to just throw it in the garbage. I've never been that type of person, especially with art. It didn't matter how creepy it was, someone had put a lot of time and effort into it. Yet, it was far too disturbing to hang up on a wall in the living room where I would see it all the time. More than just disturbing, I seemed to be having a physical reaction to it like I had never felt before. A growing knot in my stomach and a rising sensation in my gorge.

I went into the kitchen and took the oven mitts from on top of the fridge, picked the portrait up with them and held it out in front of me as if it was radioactive. I brought it down to the basement of my house and set the giant frame down against a wall on the floor, thinking I would leave it there for a while (until I got used to it?), telling myself, out of sight, out of mind.

There was no way to get it out of my thoughts, though. I kept seeing the woman's face every time I blinked. Her glassy black eyes and too-wide grin. I couldn't sleep that night, thinking about her down below me in the basement.

I felt like I could almost hear her moving around down there. The gentle creak of her footsteps stepping quietly across the floorboards. But that was impossible, I told myself. Those things were impossible.

Still, I didn't sleep. Not even for a second.

*

The following night I went down to the basement to do laundry (after building up the courage all day to go down there) and I walked past the painting. The woman's stern black eyes seemed to follow me as I went by. Her entire body was cloaked in shadow, the gloomy details of her face barely visible in the portrait's low light.

It was late at night and I lived alone, so I was more than a bit freaked out when I heard something loudly topple over when I turned my back to her, causing a shiver to run up my spine. I dropped the laundry basket and spun around to look.

She was staring at me from her place in the portrait. She had not moved, and yet her eyes seemed to be following me, the faintest movement barely noticeable with the naked eye. There was something else, too.

A box had toppled over, spilling its contents on the chair beside the painting. And yet I had not stepped anywhere near enough to disturb it.

The woman's smile seemed to have grown wider as well - crooked teeth starting to peek out from underneath her broken, bloody lips (had those looked like that before?). But maybe that was just my imagination. I decided not to look closer. I imagined her suddenly climbing out of the painting as I leaned in to inspect it, crawling out of the frame like the girl in "The Ring," and racing towards me quickly on all fours.

Shaking that image from my mind, I picked up the bin again and reluctantly turned away. I quickly put the laundry in the washing machine and turned it on, then walked past her again on my way back upstairs.

There was no mistaking it. Her grin had stretched wider, and beneath that I saw a long row of teeth - dirty, crooked, and utterly inhuman. I was very sure it hadn't looked like that before. Was I seeing things due to my lack of sleep?

I wiped my eyes and blinked, examining the painting again.

No teeth. And yet I had been so sure a second earlier.

Unable to stand looking at it for one more moment, I decided to do something.

My heart was beating rapidly in my chest and my hand was shaking as I reached down and flipped the painting around, so that it faced the wall. Her smile seemed to shrink a little bit, her eyes following my hand, brows furrowing as she looked up at me reaching over her to grab the top of the picture frame.

My skin crawled again when I touched it. I fought through the urge to retch and spun it around quickly as if it would burn me if I held on for too long.

When she was facing the wall I felt no better, only more uneasy, as if I had turned my back on a deadly enemy.

*

Again that night, I heard someone in the basement moving around. Walking from room to room.

I was just glad she didn't come up the stairs. But I had a feeling she would, and soon.

That whole night I stayed awake, listening for the footsteps. Every so often I would hear them, and every so often there would be a titter of muffled laughter, bemused and unsettling.

*

The next morning I called a friend over. I needed someone else to look at it. To make me feel less alone, I suppose. I was hoping the presence of another person would make things better somehow. But I was wrong.

My friend Brent came by and I brought him down to the basement immediately. He took one look at the painting (which was now mysteriously tipped over, facing upwards), then walked straight out of the room, saying, "NOPE!"

He went back up the stairs and out the front door of the house, much to my amazement. I followed him and stood with him on the front steps. Brent was out there with his hands on his knees, bent over and looking oddly out of breath.

But then I realized he wasn't just short of breath, he was completely terrified.

"Where the hell did you g-g-get that thing?" he asked, his speech fast and stuttering. "Y-y-you can't keep it. You can't! It's evil! Possessed!! It looked right at me! How can you s-s-s-sleep with that thing in your house?"

Brent hadn't stuttered since back in elementary school, except the odd time when he was really stressed out. He'd seen speech language experts for years and had eventually cured himself of the speech disorder. It only came out when he was really upset.

"I haven't. I haven't slept a wink since I got that thing."

He looked me dead in the eyes.

"GET RID OF IT."

I told him I would, with every intention of throwing it in the trash or burning it after he left. But for some strange reason I could not.

I decided I had to do something with it first. I had to find out some answers.

*

The next day, after another restless night of tossing and turning, I brought the painting out to my car. We were going to go for a little drive together.

I had wrapped it up in a blanket and the portrait was covered up so nobody could see it. Mostly because I didn't want to look at it. Especially while I was driving.

There was an art expert about two hours drive away from my house. I had looked him up online and found he was a well-established authority on all things creepy and disturbing. It had taken a while to find someone with his reputation. The better part of the previous day, in fact.

While I drove, I looked back at the painting in the rear view mirror occasionally. From underneath the blankets, I could have sworn I saw subtle movement. The bend and ripple of the sheet kept catching my eye and distracting me from the road ahead.

It could have been the wind, but it wasn't. I was certain of it.

*

"You've got yourself quite an antique, by the looks of it," the man said, beginning to pull back the blanket to reveal the gilded frame.

I realized I was holding my breath, closing my eyes, waiting for his reaction when he saw the horrifying woman in the portrait. But when he finally gasped in astonishment, I realized it was not a fearful sound, but one of admiration.

"Remarkable…"

Opening my eyes, I looked at what he was seeing. The face of the woman in the portrait was not the same - I did a double take and wondered for a moment if he had switched them out when I wasn't paying attention. But no, it was the same frame, the same woman in the portrait. Only her expression had changed remarkably.

Instead of the horrifying smile, she now wore a benign look on her face - a passive, good natured smirk that I was unaccustomed to seeing on her.

"Magnificent chiaroscuro. That's a technique which involves heavy-handed use of shadows and darkness with little light, in case you aren't familiar. But the brush strokes, my goodness! Utterly invisible," he said, holding up a loop to examine it closely. "It looks as if she's alive! Someone went to a lot of trouble to make this. Do you have the provenance?"

"The prova-what?" I should have known the word - did, in fact, but was far too tired to remember what it meant at that moment. I'd now gone nearly four full days without sleep and was dead on my feet.

"Any idea of its origins, or its age?"

"No, sorry. I got it online at this site," I said, pulling out my phone and trying to show him. But the website no longer existed as far as I could tell. "Weird, I guess it's down right now. I'll send you the URL."

He thought about it for a few minutes, going over the painting with various tools and magnifying lenses.

"Ah, here's something!" he said excitedly.

"What's that?" I asked.

"Damn, I can only see part of the signature - I'll have to take it out of the frame. Can you leave it with me until tomorrow?"

I agreed, unsure of how to explain to him the situation other than to say, "Be careful with it."

In retrospect, I guess I should have. I should have at least tried.

Poor bastard.

*

The art expert didn't pick up the phone the following day and I thought maybe he just needed more time with the piece. But inside I knew something was very wrong already.

I had slept for the first time in four nights, though - no longer hearing the footsteps creaking on the floorboards beneath me anymore. And I wanted one more night of peace before hearing the truth from the man I'd left the picture with. Selfish, I know. In retrospect, I was just terrified to go back there. Who knew what I would find?

After one more night of rest, I called the art expert again and once more I received no answer, no call back.

Getting worried for the old guy now, I got in my car and started driving first thing in the morning - I didn't eat breakfast, feeling like I would throw it up if I did. Despite the lack of food in my belly it felt like there was a cinder block sitting inside of it the whole drive there.

I just hoped he was okay.

*

When I arrived at the man's studio, I found the front door was unlocked.

I entered the small foyer and found it dark and empty inside. He did not come out to greet me this time, and the sense of dread I was feeling continued to grow and swell inside of me.

With slow, careful steps, I began to walk through the foyer towards the door where his studio was kept. That was where I had last left him and I hoped that I would open the door to find him standing there, working on something. I no longer cared about the painting - in fact I hoped that he had destroyed it in my absence, that way I wouldn't have to do it.

The last two nights had given me a clearer mind and the sleep had afforded me perspective and insight into the situation. The thing had to be destroyed - but it had some power over me which had prevented me from doing so - I had been tricked into hanging onto it and showing it to more and more people.

Pushing open the door marked, "Studio," I went inside the next dark room.

"Hello," I called out in the blackened space.

A soft gurgling noise responded. It sounded bubbly and wet.

I reached over to turn on the light, but found it no longer worked. The room stayed drenched in darkness. And then I heard that same familiar titter of laughter I had heard from my basement. HER.

My heart now pounding in my chest, I swallowed a dry lump in my throat. Reaching for my phone, I pulled it out and tried with trembling fingers to turn on the flashlight app.

My hands were shaking so badly I dropped the phone. I bent down to pick it up and heard movement in the darkness. It was getting closer. There was another sound as well, a soft drip, drip, drip like a leaky roof, only coming from several different places.

Picking up the phone from the floor, I managed to unlock it as I felt a presence move past me in the darkness. The air around me suddenly felt cold as a winter's night and I found myself shivering and shaking even more as I finally got the flashlight turned on.

The light came on, casting the room in its harsh white glow.

Chiaroscuro.

A grotesque sort of art exhibit had been created in the studio, but not by the resident art expert who I had met two days prior. No, he had not made this monstrosity, but he was certainly a part of it.

The whole room was filled with his entrails, strung up and down and across the perimeter like party streamers. He was at the center of it all. His body had been disemboweled and his guts had been pulled out and wrapped around the room. His limbs had been removed as well, but were nowhere to be seen.

That was when I saw the most horrifying part. He was still somehow alive. His mouth opened and closed like a fish out of water, his skin partially missing from his face, revealing stark white bone beneath, ligaments and tendons.

"HMMOOH?" came from his mouth and I noticed his tongue had been removed as well, and blood was pouring out, causing him to cough and choke occasionally.

The walls had been painted with his blood, which was everywhere. Various symbols which I did not recognize were on every inch of the room, ceilings, floors, and walls. They looked druidic and ancient - their meanings unknown to me.

As I looked around, I remembered the noise I had heard by the door. I spun and saw her standing there in the darkness. The woman from the painting. She was dressed in a dark robe and her grin was wider than ever, large and open with silent laughter. Blood was smeared around her mouth. In her hand, she held the painting itself, only she was no longer in it. The background was black and empty, now missing its subject.

Realizing suddenly what was happening, I noticed that her entrancing eyes were coming towards me. She was coming towards me. How long had I been standing there, zoned out? The only thing, which had snapped me out of it was the gurgling screams of the art expert, sounding desperate and terrified.

She held the picture frame out in front of her as if to capture me in it.

My heart beating fast, I did the only thing I could think to do. I shone the flashlight straight in her eyes, hoping it would be her weakness. A creature borne of the shadows and of the darkness - I thought maybe the light would do something to stop her.

It worked! The second the glare hit her eyes she put her hands up to shield her face, covering it with the picture frame. But her hands continued to burn and sizzle like a vampire in the sun.

Still, she continued moving toward me. Terrified, I backed up, tripping over a chair and falling to the floor. The phone fell from my hand and clattered away, in the direction of the art expert. His face was lit up, looking at me in its harsh glow.

"VAH SMITCH!" he yelled, struggling to speak without a tongue, looking close to death from blood loss.

He was looking at the wall and I could see a light switch there. Struggling to my feet, I saw she was nearly on top of me and heard her quietly whispering some sort of prayer or chant under her breath. I ducked away just as she brought down the portrait where my head was a moment before.

I had the feeling if I hadn't gotten out of the way I would be stuck inside that painting now, just like she had been.

In the dull light I managed to find the light switch on the nearby wall with my hand and flicked it on, casting the entire room in harsh white artificial light.

The woman from the painting screamed, her skin boiling and steaming in the glow of the fluorescents. Boils and blisters bloomed and burst on her skin, pus and blood running out in rivulets.

Covering her face with her robes, she ran to the door and fled just as she was about to catch fire, judging by the looks of it.

I hoped she would leave, but she didn't. Her footsteps stopped just outside the door.

She's still out there in the foyer. Waiting for me in the darkness. Waiting for the sun to go down. Waiting for me to try and leave. I can hear her pacing as she waits for me to come out - the next subject for her painting.

The art expert is dead now, he stopped breathing a few minutes ago. It's just me left - with his bloody guts strewn around the room and strung up like a giant intestinal spider web all around me. The drip, drip, drip begins to slow down as his blood coagulates.

And the blood-painted symbols on the walls begin to move and shift and morph as the one working fluorescent bulb in the room flickers and suddenly goes out.

I really wish I'd just burned that damn painting.

The Google Algorithm is Beginning to Scare Me

The Google algorithm has been acting up lately. It has been giving me very strange recommendations.

Usually it's right on the money and sometimes predicts things that I want before I have even mentioned them out loud and I wonder how it knows. Is it reading my mind? Or does it just know me better than I know myself?

For instance, recently I was thinking about replacing my laptop. The old one was starting to malfunction and was slowing down to the point of being irritating. Surely enough, ads for laptops started appearing at the side of my browser window when I visited various websites – even though I hadn't mentioned the problem to anyone and hadn't even said out loud that the old laptop was bothering me.

Again and again, ads began to show up that catered to my very exact needs – getting more and more creepily specific. A hole ripped suddenly in my underwear – and an ad for underwear popped up on my Google phone. I broke a coffee mug – and ads for coffee mugs started to show up. I didn't even have to think about stuff after a while, it popped up on my feed before I even knew I wanted it.

I tried not to give in to these temptations, but I couldn't help myself. The ads were too perfect. It was everything I ever needed at the click of a button. It didn't help that I had a shopping addiction once upon a time - this brought it all back.

The bills began to pile up as my online shopping became a real problem for my wife and I financially. I started seeing looks of disgust and annoyance on her face when she talked to me, and I realized I was ruining our marriage with my constant need for these perfect new things which were clearly meant so specifically just for me.

But to be honest it wasn't just that, there were problems long before that. The buying habit was just an escape, I had begun to realize.

Still, I couldn't let her take that from me. She wanted to cut up my credit card, and wanted to cancel it. But I told her no.

Then, very soon after that, new ads started to appear when I was browsing on the laptop. Ads for shovels. For lye. For dark clothing and flashlights. For spades, pickaxes, and grass seed.

Strange, I thought at first, since we didn't even live in a house with a backyard. Why was it making such odd recommendations all of a sudden?

Looking at the laptop more closely, I realized why the algorithm had my desires wrong suddenly. I wasn't synced to my Google account. The laptop was logged into my wife's profile.

But why would she want to buy those items? Gardening tools don't make a lot of sense when you don't have a garden, or even a yard.

I opened up the history tab, going back and seeing what she had been looking at. Strangely, the last 24 hours were wiped blank.

She was still out at the grocery store, so I pulled up the bank statements and her credit card account, overwhelmed with a desire to find out the truth, like an itch in my mind that I couldn't help but scratch.

When I logged into my Google account and tried to "follow the money" as they always say in movies, I couldn't help but notice the new ads dominating the borders of my computer screen.

"Learn Self Defence NOW! Meadow Valley Karate School – currently accepting new students"

"Put on these brand new NIKE running shoes and get outside! GO!"

And then, finally...

"Bob's gun store – You can't put a price on safety!"

That last one was actually nearby, and so I decided to quit browsing the internet and just get out of the house. After all, the only thing I could find in our bank and credit card history was a big cash withdrawal the day prior. It hadn't been me, only Christine could have taken the money out. But why?

Part of me wasn't surprised when I saw her car parked outside of the gun store. She was so transfixed by her new purchase that she didn't even notice me as I drove past, gawking at her.

She was holding a large pistol in her hand and stroking it thoughtfully. Christine had always said she hated guns. I guessed maybe that she had changed her mind.

I drove for a long time after that, more afraid than I had ever felt in my life. Terrified of the woman I had married.

A couple hours outside of the city my phone started to ring.

I pulled over onto the gravel shoulder and fished the Google Pixel phone out of my pocket with shaking hands, looking at the screen. It was a video call from Christine. She was obviously wondering where I was.

Swiping up on the screen, I saw her face appear. Seeing it made me feel like I had been wrong about everything. Like it had all been a big mistake. She could never do anything to hurt me.

"Hey, where are you? Are you driving?" I asked her, seeing the background of her video call. She looked to be on a country road somewhere.

"Yeah, of course! I was worried sick about you! I pulled up your GPS data on your phone because you didn't come home for dinner. Where are you going?"

Of course, I had forgotten about that. She knew my passwords and could track my phone.

"Tell him to stay where he is," a man's voice said in the background.

"Stay where you are, I'm coming to get you, okay?"

She was coming to get me, alright.

"Christine, whose voice was that?"

The call suddenly cut out as her stunned face seemed unable to come up with a response to my question.

I'm browsing my phone now, looking for a motel where I can spend the night.

The promoted ones that keep popping up are for places in Mexico.

I think maybe I should listen to Google this time.

There is Life on Mars - We Just Woke it up

The frigid, wind-swept surface of Mars has a thin atmosphere. It is constantly bombarded with deadly radiation from above. The air is toxic, the soil is poisonous, and there's little benefit in setting up a traditional basecamp there as had been done on the moon. For us to survive more than a few years on our top secret advance scouting mission, we had to build down, not up. And so we made our base below ground.

Unfortunately for us, there was something else down there with us, in the caverns below the surface. Something that had been lying dormant and forgotten in the darkness.

And we woke it up.

*

Kate was swinging her pickaxe against the wall, breaking off chunks of loose rock. The ceaseless ringing sound of metal on stone was echoing and constant in the dim space. I once found it annoying, but I was so used to it now that it didn't even register. It helped that on Mars sound didn't work the same way. Things were duller, quieter there.

The headlamps on either side of my helmet illuminated a wide region in front of me as I worked, shoveling rocks into a wheelbarrow. Everything else was blanketed in darkness. Even on the surface light was only a third of what it would be on earth. Underground the darkness was actually oppressive. It felt like you were drowning in it.

Suddenly I heard a noise like the wall had just caved in behind me where she was standing. A loud showering of rocks falling over suddenly, and I wheeled around to see Kate was gone. Just gone.

I moved as quickly as I could in that direction, maneuvering in the low gravity with my bulky suit encumbering every step. Running over to where she had been, I called for help, asking the others in the main living quarters to come quickly.

There was a hole in the rock where Kate had been. When I finally got close enough to see what happened, I looked into the gap and saw a vast and dark cavernous space behind the rock wall. My headlamp shone through and I looked down to see Kate struggling on the treacherous terrain where she'd fallen. She'd slid a little ways down a steep hill made of crumbling dirt and rocks. The loose ground was slipping beneath her feet as she attempted desperately to gain purchase.

"I need some help!" she cried, trying and failing to find her footing. The angle was so steep she was clearly struggling, trying not to show the terror on her face.

"I got you, Kate," I tried, my words sounding false to my own ears. "Just hang on."

But I saw that she couldn't hang on. She was being swallowed up by the blackness below, more and more by the second. She was almost ten feet down the slope now and too far for me to grab her. Then fifteen feet, then twenty.

"Bring ropes and climbing equipment!" I called to the others in the habitation unit. "Double-time, guys, hurry, Kate's in trouble!"

They responded affirmative on the radio.

I watched horrified as she slid further and further down into the darkness below.

"Hang on, Kate! Now, guys! We need you out here now!!"

Behind her I could see there was a huge underground cavern. My lamp could not illuminate far enough to see the floor or the other end of it. The dark space had to be massive, considering the NASA head lamps were top-of-the-line. The high-powered beam of light cut through the blackness for a ways and then was swallowed up.

When I looked down again, Kate was gone. She didn't respond on her radio, either. The sound of her impact to the floor below did not come back up to me, and I imagined her falling slowly in the low gravity at first, her descent quickly increasing, faster and faster until she reached a deadly velocity and then it wouldn't matter anymore how forgiving the gravity was.

But the sound of her impact never came.

Wei and Reed ran out of the air-lock with ropes in hand, looking at me with concern. I waved them over and pointed down into the blackness below.

"This section is hollow, she broke right through with the pickaxe. She fell in and couldn't climb back up. It's all crumbling rocks so I think she must have slid right down. But how far, I'm not sure."

Captain Reed seemed to consider the options. Time was of the utmost importance – if she was still alive down there her air supply would be limited.

We all stared through the hole into the blackness and looked up to see the roof of the cavern far above. It was very odd, since our bunker was next to a large vertical rock face that we'd always assumed was sturdy and solid. Now we realized the giant mountain of stone right behind our base was hollow, like the fossilized skull of an ancient colossus. It seemed unnatural to my eyes. But I'm no geologist.

Wei quickly went in to call back to base as I looked down helplessly into the dark abyss of the cavern.

"...ello? Nathan are you..."

The radio crackled with static but I could hear her voice in my helmet.

"Kate? Are you okay? Can you hear me?"

There was nothing for a few moments then I heard the static crackle again.

"..es, I can hear you! Can you he..."

I waited but there was only silence once again.

"You're cutting out. How far down are you? We can lower a rope."

"There's something down here, Nathan… I can't explain it but… pool of water that broke my fall…"

"Kate? Did you say water!?"

Nothing after that again for a few minutes, despite trying again multiple times.

We all stared at each other, dumbfounded.

The average temperature on the surface of mars is approximately -46 degrees Celsius. It was much colder than that in the caverns where we were located, away from the sun's warming rays. Far too cold for liquid water. We were protected from the deadly radiation present on the surface, though, and that was the major benefit of being below ground.

"She must have a concussion or a head injury. Someone's going to have to go down there, I think."

"I'll go," I volunteered immediately.

Putting on the climbing harness, I tried to put one leg at a time through the loops of woven fabric, the way I had done a thousand times, still I found myself struggling. My hands were shaking and I couldn't get my fingers to work properly.

Finally I got the damn thing on and attached the other clips and ropes and equipment to my suit. Reed handed me two climbing axes as well, just in case.

I lowered myself slowly over the side of the steep cliff edge and made my way down.

The darkness surrounded me on all sides as I went deeper and deeper down, feeling suffocated by blackness. I had to remind myself to breathe.

It felt like I was descending downwards forever as the light above got dimmer and eventually disappeared entirely. The walls looked yellow and strange, veiny and organic when I shone my lights on them, but I didn't have time to stop and look, just assumed it was an unusual type of rock formation.

As I dropped down further my head began to feel light, my vision suddenly blurred for a moment and I had trouble seeing.

Then it cleared again and my ears began to ring painfully. I didn't understand what was happening and started to hear voices whispering in my ears instead of ringing, until it seemed as if they were right inside my mind, speaking to me. But in a tongue I did not understand and that was not human.

No, that can't be right.

Finally Kate's headlights became visible. I saw she was standing down below and was touching the surface of the rock wall. But it was not a rock wall, I realized with dawning apprehension.

The walls were moving and shifting, they were covered in yellow web-like formations that I saw were everywhere. All over the floors and walls and ceiling of this unnatural chamber, so close to me I could examine them as I finished dropping down to the floor below. The yellow webs looked familiar for some reason and it took me a few moments to realize why.

The yellow web-like formations were almost identical to slime mold. One of the most curious and interesting lifeforms on planet Earth. Of course not known to exist on mars. Coincidentally I knew a thing or two about the stuff.

Slime mold is not a fungus. It is not an animal or a plant. It is separate from everything else on the tree of life. Almost as if it has its own tree of life. It grows to be very large (up to several feet in diameter - but nothing like this) and it's a single-celled organism, except with millions of nuclei. And it is potentially capable of some form of intelligence. In labs they have found that slime mold can solve mazes, for instance.

And they grow extremely quickly. They can expand and contract like the muscles in our own bodies, using a vaguely similar mechanism.

Thinking about these things in the back of my mind, I couldn't help but feel afraid as my feet touched the stone floor and I saw the yellow slime was on me immediately, quickly growing and expanding onto my boots, moving much faster than anything seen on earth. I called out over the radio to Kate once again. She was standing right in front of me but did not turn around.

I began to approach her and looked down to see the strands of yellow webbing sticking and stretching from the bottom of my feet. It was like walking across a movie theater floor covered in gum, each step difficult and taxing.

Finally I reached her and put my hand on her shoulder. She spun around quickly and I saw her eyes were surprised and blinking as if I had just awoken her from sleep.

"Kate? Can you hear me?"

"Oh. Nathan. Hi."

There was a crack in the glass of her helmet and some of the yellow slime mold was oozing around it. With dawning horror I realized that it was actually inside her helmet, moving around and exploring the space. Some was on her neck as well and in her hair and I nearly gagged with unexplainable revulsion at the sight of it on her.

"Kate. You have a breach in your suit. We need to get you back to the lab."

"We can't go yet, Nathan. Look at all this." She was speaking softly as if she was sleepwalking, her voice a lilting lullaby, everything she said in a sing-song tone, quietly and at a whisper. I wanted to ask her why she was talking like that, why she wasn't listening to common sense, but more than anything I just wanted to get away.

I know that must sound awful, but part of me wanted desperately, more than anything, just to get the hell away from her and away from that yellow slime mold-looking stuff that didn't belong there.

"Kate, we have to go, please. Come on."

"They're talking to me, Nathan. Do you hear them too? If you listen closely you can almost make out the words. I'm even starting to understand them, Nathan."

I tried to grab her arm and she pushed me away, turning her face to look at me angrily as she did so. "DON'T TOUCH ME." Turning around, I saw the 'pool of water' that she had described falling into. It was not water at all, but a large deposit of the yellow slime mold in a large crater nearby, bubbling and moving around. Whipping tendrils stuck out from it curiously and darted around, seeming to inspect the air.

"Bring me back up," I said over the radio. "Kate's refusing assistance. There's some strange organism growing down here and she's… uh, not done with it yet."

Or it's not done with her.

They didn't seem to hear me over the radio so I simply pulled twice on the rope and they began to reel me back in.

It didn't feel right, leaving Kate down there, but I told myself I didn't have a choice. We'd have to regroup and come up with a plan. Maybe she would listen to Reed if he went down and ordered her to return.

The darkness swallowed her up beneath me and I looked down at my boots in dismay to see that the yellow webbed slime mold was hanging on to me still, wriggling and squirming and exploring my legs.

It appeared to be searching desperately for a way into my suit.

Bewildered and confused, my mind grappled with a hundred different scenarios, still in shock over what we had just discovered.

There was life on Mars. Disgusting, slimy, potentially telepathic life. But, still. For the first time in history it had just been irrefutably proven beyond any doubt. I had just witnessed a never-before-seen breed of what I assumed was slime mold growing in the depths of the cavern. Somehow it was still alive and thriving despite extreme temperatures and an absence of any known food supply. The whole thing existed beyond science and logic, and yet it was there.

My crew wouldn't believe me, I thought to myself, if not for the remnants of it clinging desperately to my boots.

They hauled me up through the opening in the rock and immediately began to ask why Kate was not with me. "She refused to come back up. There's something down there, a kind of organism. This stuff," I said, pointing at my boots.

"What the hell is that!?" Wei exclaimed. She was normally calm and composed but now she was backing away, stumbling over rocks and shaking. "I can hear it in my head!"

Reed began to look concerned as well and I remembered how something similar had happened to me as I had descended down into the cavern. I had nearly dismissed the voices in my head as my imagination and fear until Kate confirmed she heard them too.

"Oh yeah, that. Just wait, it'll pass," I said, hoping it would as it had for me.

After a few long moments it did.

"What the hell are we dealing with here?" Reed asked.

I only wished I could give him an answer.

The three of us went back inside for a brief rest and to regroup. Wei went straight to her lab with an odd look on her face, saying she'd examine the slime mold and try to give us some answers. She'd also communicate with home base from there and explain the newest developments, via an uplink in her lab.

Reed and I stood pacing in the habitation unit's kitchen/dining area debating what the hell we were going to do. Kate had refused to come back up with me and I told him she didn't seem to be herself. It was like the slime mold stuff was telling her to stay there. I didn't understand it but there it was.

"We can't convince her to come up, right? Which leaves us exactly one option as far as I'm concerned. We hitch a rope to her suit and drag her back up here. I don't like it but it's what we've gotta do."

After a bit more discussion the two of us decided I would go down again while Reed stayed up top, since he was the strongest. It was easy enough to pull a person up in the low gravity, but two was another story altogether. If necessary I told him I would wait down below while he pulled Kate up and then he could send the rope back down again afterwards.

Going down into the darkness again was even more terrifying that the first time. Even though I knew slightly what to expect, the whole thing was going wrong, I could tell already when I heard Wei's voice speaking over the radio.

She was speaking in a whispering lullaby tone, the same as Kate.

"We don't need to bring her back up here, Captain Reed," she said. "Tell Nathan to come back up."

"I don't understand. Can you repeat, Wei?"

"She must stay down below. Mother is hungry and must eat. Mother must become one."

I didn't like the sounds of that one bit.

"Reed, you need to bring me back up. Wei is compromised. She's talking like that thing is controlling her, like it was controlling Kate!"

"She's coming out here, Nathan. She's got a knife. Oh God. Get back! Get back! Stop, please, Wei... Listen to me..." He cut out abruptly.

The rope I was holding suddenly began to drop in sickening lurches. I fell ten feet, then twenty, feeling sick as I bounced back up with the sudden tension. Gravity pulled me back down and I held on to the rope desperately, feeling that I was about to die for certain.

Beneath me the ground came into view and I saw Kate's light now shining dimly from the wall, but I did not see her. The rope dropped again as Reed was attacked by the thing above, the thing that had once been Wei now clearly trying to kill him judging by the sounds of it and judging by how he was holding the rope, or not holding it.

This time I fell all the way to the floor below, slowly at first, then faster and faster as the ground sped towards me. I landed awkwardly, twisting my ankle, and called out in pain.

Looking over my shoulder, I saw the rope was still there, hanging from the cliff above. So Reed was still up there, hanging on for dear life and fighting off Wei or whatever she had become. I only hoped he was alright.

Then I turned around and saw Kate, or what was left of her. She was enveloped by the wall she had been standing in front of when I left her. Her face stared out at me and I saw the yellow webbed slime was now covering her eyes and nose, it was in her ears and worst of all it went into her mouth like an intubation device, going down her throat. Blackish-yellow veins lined her face and neck and her entire space suit was wrapped in sticky yellow-webbed slime which held her fastened tightly to the wall.

Despite my terror I found myself stepping forward, wanting to help her still, somehow wanting to do the right thing and get her out of there. If only I could clip the rope to her suit… At that thought the webbing seemed to unravel and released her like a Venus Fly Trap letting go of its prey, like a flower opening in bloom. Though her face was covered with yellow slime she walked towards me as if she could see me through it. The oozing webs stretched out behind her as she came at me. That's when I realized the voice in my head telling me to stay and save her was not my own. It was a foreign voice speaking in a close approximation of my own thoughts, telling me not to worry, telling me to remain calm, to stay, to become one.

I ran instead.

The rope was still there and that was enough for me. I grabbed onto it and began to climb, my feet walking up the side of the steep vertical cliff as quickly as I could. I didn't dare to look back, but knew that Kate was just behind me. Not Kate, but what was left of her.

Struggling up the sheer 90 degree slope, I found myself tiring more and more. The wall seemed as if it was grabbing onto my feet and wrapping them up in webs with every step I took, getting stronger and pulling harder all the time.

The strands of yellow slime grabbed on and refused to let go, snapping in half only with great effort on my part. I pulled myself up the rope and walked up through the living muck as it tried tenaciously to hold onto me. All the while as I walked up the wall I heard whispering in my mind, louder and louder now. Every so often I would find my hands beginning to let go of the rope without any conscious effort on my part, and had to fight off the voices and tell myself to hang on. Even though they spoke in a language unknown to me it seemed not to matter, as their will was made known to my mind and I had to fight from bowing to its growing power.

Finally I reached the top and pulled myself back into the light. The habitation unit was visible just ahead and I saw that the rope was tied off haphazardly to the door handle.

Captain Reed was lying on the dirt floor of the underground space where all of this mess began. His helmet was cracked and his face was bloodied but he was still alive. Wei was lying next to him, a knife protruding from her chest. "I had to," he began, seeming unsure how to continue. "She came at me and tried to kill me. I barely managed to get the rope tied off…"

With dawning horror I realized I had not pulled the rope up after me. I ran over to the ledge and looked down to see Kate climbing up. She was only a little ways down, the yellow slime mold covering her eyes and mouth like a slimy yellow-webbed bridal veil.

Terrified, I backed away, realizing there was no time to cut the rope or stop her, she was almost at the top. As her hands grabbed the ledge, I looked down to see Captain Reed telling me to go, to run. I hurried inside through the air-lock and slammed the door behind me. I hastily got my suit off and ran to the computer to change the access code for entry. Luckily I was quick with the keyboard and managed to secure the only access point just as the creature that was once Kate started to hammer on the door.

I looked out through the small window and saw her, covered in yellow slime, which writhed and pulsated. The webbed mold was growing everywhere now, on every surface she touched. It expanded outwards at an alarming speed.

It spread over Wei's body and I saw it break off her head at the neck like a drumstick from a chicken. Hungrily, it dove in through the bottom of the helmet and began to consume. With incredible strength, other parts of the webbed slime wrapped around her legs and broke them apart at the joints, the white bone, muscle and blood spilling out before being devoured.

As the mass continued to grow and spread, malignant and out of control, it reached Captain Reed. His face was a mask of terror and I held the door with white-knuckled fury unable to turn away as it broke him in half. The yellow tendrils broke his ribcage open and gushed in like a wave crashing on the beach, taking everything.

In my headset I could hear him screaming until very suddenly I couldn't anymore. Turning away, I slumped down to the floor and sat, waiting for it to be over.

I've been trapped inside for quite a while now. I sent this communication back to base and everyone thinks I've gone insane, that I've perhaps killed the rest of the crew and am now trying to blame mind-controlling space mold. As if I couldn't come up with a better story than that.

I mean, really. The soil is toxic here. The air is unbreathable. There are a million and one ways to die here and if I needed to find an excuse for the death of my crew... Well, I'd find a better one than this.

Luckily one or two people believe me. They've agreed to get this out there, at least in some fashion.

As for me, I wait. It's already inside the habitation unit. I was too careless when I took off my suit. Now it's starting to grow all over, starting to spread.

It's on me now, moving up my legs and my fingers and arms, fine tendrils of yellow branching out slowly and insidiously. Infecting me. Making me part of the one. It tickles my throat as it spreads spore-like downwards, like a black mold growing quietly in a dark, wet corner of a bathroom. It grows.

The thing that was once Kate watches me from the window in the door, waiting. Whispering.

In my mind she's whispering to me now. In a sing-song tone telling me to open the door. And all the while it's spreading.

Can you hear it?

Mankind should've Stayed Far Away from Mars

The first manned mission to Mars began well enough.

Launched without the knowledge of the general public, it lasted for almost a decade, silencing the naysayers in NASA and abroad. It was by all measures a success, until a series of unfortunate events occurred. These unexplained phenomena brought the entire project to a crashing halt.

All contact was lost after nine years of successful habitation on the red planet. Something tragic had happened to the crew and at least one of them had seemingly gone insane. It was suspected that Science Officer Nathan Flanders had killed the rest of the astronauts on the mission and had taken his own life following his final transmission.

That's where the four of us came in.

We were sent to conduct a salvage operation and tasked with surviving against all odds on the barren planet's surface. Instructions were to use what we could from the old base – the multi-billion dollar array of advanced equipment was invaluable and some of it was reportedly irreplaceable.

Our flight and landing on the surface went well, proceeding without incident. Despite that our nerves were on edge and the four of us were jittery with anticipation as we made our way from the landing craft to the hatch which led to the underground habitation unit.

The area surrounding us looked surprisingly similar to Earth – a desolate desert region scattered with flat rocks and boulders – and a sheer wall of rock that jutted out from the ground upwards stood just behind the old habitation unit's coordinates.

We bounded toward the hatch, stumbling awkwardly in the lower gravity. I felt occasional moments of success when a step forward was executed just right, but otherwise my ambulation was awkward and clumsy. I fell over at one point and bounced back up after a couple attempts. There was a smile stretching across my face, though, and I looked over to see Denise was doing the same. We couldn't help it. We were fulfilling a lifelong dream and despite or maybe because of the tension of the situation we began to grin like idiots and laugh.

Finally, we reached our destination. Raymond pried open the hatch door. Dust and sand poured off the flat surface as he heaved it open. Clearly it had been a while since anyone had gone down there, into the pitch blackness below. The idea anyone was still alive in the habitation unit was unlikely if not impossible, but we we'd prepared for nearly any situation.

 There had been enough food and water supply for one man to survive and we were told there was a slim chance we would be forced to defend ourselves if compromised crew members were still alive down there.

Last contact had been with Nathan Flanders – the failed mission's science officer. He had claimed there was something down below, in the area being dug out for the base's expansion, some sort of organism, and that it had infected the crew.

He had called it "telepathic slime mold" according to reports.

Ridiculous, of course. Nothing could live in the freezing temperatures of the caverns beneath the surface of Mars. It was far too cold for that.

But the rationale for that specific delusion made some sense – Flanders had researched slime mold extensively during his formative academic years, so it seemed to follow logically that he would revert back to thinking about it during a mental break. At least that was what the psychoanalysts back at base thought. That there was some traumatic event underlying all of this that he had failed to disclose on his psych report.

As we climbed down into the habitation unit I began to suspect that we had been wrong to think he had been lying. That we had been wrong about everything. Whispering voices were speaking in my mind but I dismissed it as nerves and adrenaline, my overworked mind playing tricks on me.

The darkness was total as we descended the ladder. By the time we got down to the floor and switched on our headlamps it was too late. The hatch slammed shut above us automatically and we looked around in horror to see the controls to open it up again had been covered by yellow, slimy webbing that writhed and pulsated as if alive.

It was disorienting and surreal and for a moment I felt like a fly who had fallen into an elaborate labyrinthine spider web. It surrounded us in spiraling whorls that enveloped everything in a many-stranded maze of stringy, striated slime mold.

All of the habitation unit and its high-tech interior was covered with the stuff. It was built up on the walls and on the ceiling, covering the floors and leaving only the ladder and the small space around the base of it open, as if waiting for us, not wanting to alert us to its presence until it was too late and we were trapped.

The yellow webs writhed and moved all around us, reaching out tendril-like towards us from the walls and stretching out to touch us.

"Oh my God... What is this?" I heard Aisha whisper breathlessly through the radio.

"He was right. It wasn't a delusion. It was all true..."

"We need to get out of here, now." The captain ignored me, moving forward despite my objections.

"Hang on," said Raymond. "We have to see if we can salvage anything. Maybe we can do something to get rid of this stuff."

At the mere mention of that, the yellow slime mold began to whip itself into a frenzy. A piercing ringing noise invaded my mind and my ears felt like someone was stabbing into them with sharp pins.

My knees buckled from the pain and I nearly fell to the floor, but the sensation subsided a few moments later and we all relaxed.

"Why do you not seem the least bit fazed by all this?" I asked Raymond, suddenly suspicious. It felt like he was the only one not even remotely surprised by the fact that Nathan Flanders had been telling the truth. There really was life on Mars. And it wasn't human.

"The three of you would never have come if you'd known the truth," he said under his breath. His words were in a monotone, not sounding like himself at all. "Besides, it was classified."

"YOU KNEW!?" I shouted at him in rage. "How could you drag us here knowing this mind-controlling slime was real!?"

As I spoke the yellow gunk was stretching, spreading and climbing up my boots towards my ankles. I tried to push it away with my hands and it got stuck to my fingers and expanded, rapidly growing up my hands and onto my wrists.

"We need to get out of here," I said, no longer caring what he was going to do. "We need to get back to the ship."

"To do what? We need this place. There's no way the four of us survive here without the equipment in this hab unit. It took over a decade to set all this up – we just came to try to pick up the pieces, remember? You want to give up on that already?"

When he said it like that I had to think twice.

"You have a plan, right? Something you didn't tell us about? Another secret you kept from us?"

A grin spread across his face: "Damn right, I do. I'm trying not to think about it too much, though. Since we're not alone in our minds anymore. Try to think about something else. Golf or something, okay? Just don't get thinking too hard about what I might be planning to do. This slime stuff ain't gonna like it."

I nodded, resigned to follow him a little further. We had come this far, after all. We continued deeper into the narrow confines of the habitation unit. The webbing reached out and I felt it touching me in places outside my suit, moving towards my helmet, but I tried not to panic. I noticed Aisha had the same calm demeanor as Ray, and wondered if she knew what we were in for as well.

"Do you think it's possible that Nathan is still alive?" Denise asked, her voice shaking.

"Doubtful."

Movement came from up ahead and I saw something in the shadows. A shape lurching forward.

The thing which came out from the next room clearly once was an astronaut – but it was not Nathan Flanders. A voice rang clearly through my mind and I heard it was a woman speaking softly. Her tone was soft and lilting, almost sing-song. I found myself wanting to go to her as I listened and looked down to see the webbed slime moving up my leg further now, almost to my midsection, crawling up my body and encasing me in it. I tried to back away but found it was difficult to move suddenly. The yellow gunk was becoming more tenacious, gripping me and holding me in place like vines.

"Won't you stay with us? Be one with us. Don't you want to be a part of something bigger than yourself?" she asked inside my mind.

Her face came out from the shadows and I saw now that her entire head was covered with the yellow webbing. It reached in from a crack in the helmet and had spun itself around her features like jaundiced cotton candy. A mask of it covered her face but it was translucent enough to see through in places.

The tendrils of yellow slime webbing had enveloped her body and it carried her across the floor towards us as if she were floating upon a cloud.

"What did you do to the rest of them?" I heard myself asking aloud.

"We needed nourishment. It was such a long sleep. But now we are well fed and looking for more hosts. If you want to live here, this is the only way. If you prefer to die, that can be arranged as well."

Raymond was reaching for something in his bag. I tried not to think about it too much, what he was planning to do.

He pulled out a weapon of some kind. I had no idea it even existed or had been brought on the journey. But then again no one had told me we would be fighting for our lives against mutant telepathic slime mold, either.

The horrifying web-covered astronaut who was coming towards us was close now, only a few meters away in the confined space.

Ray squeezed the trigger and the gun let out a blast of reddish-white light like a wide laser beam. It went past our attacker, missing wide.

She was closing in now, the webbing bringing her towards us like a wicked chariot.

He fumbled in his bag for something and pulled out a small square box. Pushing a button on the gun, it ejected a smoking cartridge and I realized he was reloading, but he had almost no time. The horrifying creature was almost within striking distance now.

Slamming the fresh battery into its slot, he pulled the trigger just as the web-covered astronaut thing was mere inches from him. The blast ripped a hole through the center of the creature and she let out a piercing scream that ripped through my mind.

It took several moments to quiet, but still lingered like my ears were ringing.

Ray pulled another fresh battery pack from his bag and changed it for the old one. It seemed the gun was single-fire and needed to be reloaded after each laser burst. Still, it was a formidable weapon. *Another top secret military project?*

The possessed astronaut woman was lying on the ground, twitching and writhing, moaning in pain. Raymond walked over towards her and pointed the weapon at her head, then pulled the trigger once again.

At point blank range it obliterated the head of the possessed astronaut, putting her out of her misery and stopping her never-ending torment.

I shuddered at the thought of having my body controlled by a parasitic creature, controlling me like a puppet. This horrifying mental image rattled me badly, especially when I looked down at my hands and feet to see them being covered by the same exact stuff.

"Enough, Ray! We're lucky to be alive after that. Now can we please get the hell out of here!?"

Raymond looked me in the eyes and loaded a fresh battery into the gun.

"Not even close. We have to keep moving. We have to get to the source of it. I have coordinates – it'll be down in the caverns below the hab unit."

"Are you insane!? We don't even know if there is a source of this madness! And even if it exists we'd never get to it. Look at this shit, it's all over our suits! Pretty soon it'll be covering our visors and we won't be able to see anything. We'll die down here like the last crew! Let's get topside now and if we're lucky the sun will kill it for us!"

Suddenly, the slime mold sprang to life again, whipping its tendrils at us and then starting to squeeze my legs painfully like Boa Constrictors. I tried to lift them up to turn around and felt like I was stuck in molasses. It took every ounce of my strength to turn away from him and start heading back towards the ladder.

"If you two want to live, I suggest you come with me. He's got a death-wish," I muttered over the radio to Denise and Aisha as I moved past them in the confined space.

They looked hesitant to leave Raymond alone down there.

Before I could get away, the webbing reached out and grabbed me with long tendrils from behind and started wrapping me up like vines. It went under my arms and around my waist, then around my neck, trying to squeeze the helmet off my head so it could get to my flesh.

"It's got me!" I screamed. "HELP!"

Denise grabbed a blade from the supply bag she was carrying and went to work sawing at the tendrils that had wrapped themselves around me.

"Hang on, I got you."

Meanwhile, Aisha moved past and caught up with Raymond, her face looking hurried and uncaring of my predicament.

"Leave them," Raymond said to her, and she nodded. They stepped over the astronaut's corpse and continued through the hab towards the back end where it led towards the caverns. To the source.

I screamed at them, cursed at them both, knowing now they had been aware all along. They had both been briefed on what had really happened here. Things that I hadn't known about until just then.

Denise was cutting at the ropes of webbing that were holding me there, but every time she cut one loose, another grabbed hold.

"It's hopeless," I said to her. "Just go. Get back to the ship and tell them what happened. Tell them this place is a lost cause. It's a death sentence for anyone who comes here."

Her face was still determined, her eyes focused. She finally got one of my arms free and handed me the knife, grabbing another from her belt.

"I'm not leaving you, so shut up and cut."

I turned my body away from the wall as she cut the strands holding my waist free. Now it was only my arm that was still wrapped up in the webbing. It pulled at me and crushed my arm painfully as I tried to pull away.

Screaming, I cut haphazardly at it, hacking and sawing with reckless abandon. Denise was cutting at another large piece and although more began to wrap around me we had the upper hand now. Slashing at them with every ounce of energy we had, I finally managed to pull myself free.

"See? Told you," Denise said, smirking. "Now come on, let's get out of this hell hole."

We were both semi-covered in the yellow webbing which was now feeling heavy and cumbersome on my legs and hands as it expanded and purposefully slowed us down, resisting our every movement.

The control panel was covered in the stuff, but I remembered suddenly from my training that there was a manual release up on the hatch door. It had been installed in the event of a power failure.

I managed to reach the ladder and looked back to see Denise just behind me. Beginning to climb was difficult, the yellow slime mold sticking to my boots and sucking me back down like wet cement. With an extreme effort I got my boot up on the first ladder rung and began to climb.

The hatch door wouldn't open at first. It didn't help that I was terrified and full of panic, suddenly forgetting all my training. I began to slam my fist against it, mad with fear, unable to focus.

Slime mold was climbing up my visor now, covering it so I couldn't see. My breathing was coming fast and I found myself hyperventilating, feeling like I was drowning in it.

Finally, my fingers found the latch and I pulled on it, feeling the satisfying click of it opening.

Sunlight spilled in as I swung it open and climbed up into the air. The yellow webbing began to retreat from the light, recoiling and peeling back from my visor like it was melting.

It preferred the darkness.

Denise and I managed to get back to the landing craft. We got back inside after making sure we had gotten rid of all the stuff from our suits. Immediately, we sent a transmission back to base, explaining what had happened.

After waiting a long while, they answered back:

Any word from Raymond and Aisha? Did they set off the device? You would have felt a tremor, like a small earthquake.

So that was their plan. Some sort of device to destroy the stuff at its source. I still didn't understand why they didn't just tell us the truth. But then I supposed I wouldn't have gone if they had. Perhaps the device was some sort of bomb that would make the organism inert and harmless. Or maybe Raymond and Aisha were going to sacrifice themselves to set it off – either way I was glad I had gotten out in time.

 I responded back to base: "No, we haven't heard from them. And we haven't felt anything yet. "

But then a moment later we did feel something. An explosion beneath us. The ground caved in below the landing vessel and we were thrown to the wall as the entire landing craft plunged down into a huge sinkhole that had just been created.

When everything settled I opened my eyes to see Raymond and Aisha staring at us through the window of the landing vessel. In the darkness the yellow slime mold still covered their suits. It was on their visors now and had found its way inside and onto their faces and into their eyes and mouths, nostrils and ears. They were being controlled by the parasitic slime mold now. It was governing their actions and they had used the device designed to destroy it to instead bring us down below, into the darkness. Where we would be vulnerable to it.

We held the doors closed as they pulled on the latch, trying to get into the ship. There was a steel rod, which we managed to wedge the door closed with, at least for now.

Still, it won't hold forever. I can already see the yellow webbing sneaking in through the edges of the door, punching through weak points in the hull and growing vine-like into our living space. It's spreading towards us steadily, to our cramped spot in a corner where we watch them encroaching.

There's still people at NASA who want the public to know the truth. To know about this cover-up. They said they'll get this out there for us, one way or another.

Because they know as well as I do…

The red planet is damned.

And the human race should NEVER return here.

The Good Samaritan

This all happened last winter. I've never talked about this with anyone except law enforcement. Even my own family doesn't know - since I couldn't bear to tell them the details. I get sick just thinking about that place. The coppery smell of blood and meat - the freezing cold. We escaped, but just barely, and the horrors we experienced will scar me for life, and I'll never fully recover.

Where do I even begin?

My girlfriend and I were heading home after dinner with my parents. The weather was worse than terrible, and a travel advisory was all over the news, but we decided to attempt the roads anyway.

"Be careful," my dad told us when we left. "They're calling for white-out conditions on Highway Six. If it gets really bad just turn around and come back, okay?"

He looked nervous, but I reassured him as best as I could.

"They always say these storms are gonna be bad, but they never really are these days. Global warming, Dad. It's gonna be fine."

But of course, it wasn't.

We got about twenty miles down the road when things started to get really bad. The narrow paved highway we were traveling on became more and more snow-covered, and the blowing flurries obscured my vision so that I couldn't see more than twenty feet in front of the car. Soon that distance narrowed to fifteen feet, then ten, until the car was moving at a crawling pace and I could no longer determine where the shoulder began or where the road ended. The ditches had disappeared as well, obscured by a wall of white, which extended high into the sky above.

"Stop! Pull over, you can't see anything! You could crash into somebody, or go into a ditch!" my girlfriend Jenny was yelling. Eventually I listened and pulled over, my heart beating fast as I tried to figure out what to do.

"Shit. Well, we can't just stay here," I said. "The car's gonna get buried in snow. Then before you know it we'll run out of gas and have no heat."

My heart was pounding fast in my chest as I tried to decide what to do.

"How much is there in the tank?"

"It's just above a quarter," I told her. "Hang on, I'm gonna hop out and take a look around."

"Be careful," she said as I opened the door and looked both ways for traffic.

On foot I could see that the ditch was just a few inches to the right of where I'd pulled over, and I'd been dangerously close to going into it. But at least I wasn't in the middle of the road where a car could come flying through and hit me at any second. Still, I didn't feel safe.

I went a few feet forward, trying to determine if there was a house or a gas station nearby where we could stop and pull into a driveway. It wasn't good to be at the side of the road like this where someone could come along and crash into us at any second. Usually I'd be scared to go knocking on a stranger's door, but these were desperate times, and I would have done that in an instant if I'd seen porch lights or something indicating a house nearby. But there was nothing.

Terrified of losing the car in the snow, I didn't dare go more than twenty feet from it, and as soon as the headlights were obscured by white and totally gone I panicked and went back to it, my heart beating even faster than before. The last thing I wanted to do was lose the vehicle in the blizzard - I'd heard stories of people dying that way.

"Did you see anything?" Jenny asked as I got back into the car, freezing cold wind and stabbing needles of snow following with me.

"Nothing. I'll try to go forward a bit more. Maybe if I roll down my window I'll be able to see better."

I put the car into drive and stuck my head out the window like a dog, my nose and cheeks freezing in the cold wind and prickling with pins and needles from the snow. It felt surreal to be driving in this weather, and extremely unsafe. All I could see was white.

After progressing another thirty feet or so, we came to a standstill again. I got out and walked a few feet before losing the car in the snow, and quickly realized it was hopeless. Without any way to see the edges of the road or anything ahead of us, we were sure to end up in a ditch. It was only a matter of time.

"What are we gonna do?" Jenny asked, looking scared.

I was ready to say something back, when suddenly I saw headlights coming toward us. They didn't look like regular car headlights. They were moving slowly, and they were high up and close together. And the chugging sound that accompanied them reminded me of something that I couldn't place right away.

Looking up at the vehicle as it pulled to a stop beside our car, I saw a man in a glass box above us that looked alien and unrecognizable in the snow. And then I realized why.

It was a man in a green John Deere tractor. He was an old farmer in overalls, with a young woman on his lap who looked sixty years younger than him. I pegged him at about eighty, and guessed she was just shy of her twentieth birthday. But she had a smile on her face, and looked content.

"You folks need some help?" He asked, opening the cabin door.

"Yeah," I said, opening my own door and getting out. "Come on, Jenny. Maybe we can use their phone to call for help."

She got out and followed after me, and we all crammed into the tractor, which smelled like spent chewing tobacco and body odor mixed with hay.

"My place is just over there," he said, hooking his thumb over his shoulder from the direction where he came. "You're welcome to stay with us and wait out the storm. You can even spend the night if you have to, there's plenty of room. But I can't promise our phone will be working. Lost reception when the power went out, maybe an hour ago."

I took out my cell phone and saw the cellular network was down too. Or maybe this was just a dead zone.

"Well, we can't thank you enough for helping us," I said. "We were starting to get really worried."

The man looked grim.

"Storm like this is nothing to mess around with. You can wind up in a ditch. Nobody will find your body for days. Sometimes not even until the Spring. And by then they'll need dental records to identify you."

I shuddered involuntarily, looking at the old man with alarm. No way I would have thought him capable of saying something like that. But, then again, one thing I've learned in my life is that people can be unpredictable.

*

When we arrived at the old man's place, I saw it was a large farmhouse with a barn out back. The details of the property beyond were obscured by snow flurries, but I thought I saw the outlines of a few other buildings as well, and maybe a silo or two. It was a decent-sized farm, and I imagined at his age he had to have help running it.

He took us inside and immediately lit a cigarello, waving out the match and tossing it into a bronze dish full of blackened embers. Then he led us further into the dimly-lit home, disappearing momentarily around a corner and out of sight. The young woman hung behind us, locking the door with a key which quietly she pocketed, then regarding us with an odd smile.

The house was old and smelled like tobacco smoke and unwashed dogs. There was a gray haze and a smell of wood fire in the air, as the two of them led us toward a door concealing a short flight of stairs which brought us to the basement.

"Come on down and join the party," he said, and I breathed a sigh of relief to see there was a group of people sitting around the room at the bottom of the stairs. We wouldn't be completely alone with this strange man and his oddly-aged partner for the entire night, at least.

"I found a couple more stragglers out there," our host said, smiling. "I'm sorry, I forgot to introduce myself. I'm Randall Mitchell. This is my Goddaughter, Lucy. And these folks are like you, all of them got stuck outside in that nasty storm."

"We're all safe thanks to you, our guardian angel," a young woman with a baby said, standing up to give the old man a hug. "I don't know how we'll ever be able to repay you for this."

The old man showed his yellow, nicotine-stained teeth.

"No repayment necessary, my dear. I'm just happy I was in a position to help. We all need each other in this world from time to time. We need to feed off of each others' goodness, not deny our basic human nature."

The old man pulled his "Goddaughter" in closer, so their hips were touching in a way that made me uncomfortable.

I saw her put her hand in his back pocket and leave it there as he smiled wider.

The woman who had been thanking him looked uncomfortable and sat back down without another word. She stared at her lap, looking deep in thought and slightly worried all of a sudden.

"Now, who wants hot chocolate? I know you two do."

Jenny and I couldn't help but nod. We were both still freezing from the outdoors, and a cup of steaming hot cocoa sounded like just what the doctor ordered.

*

We introduced ourselves to the other people in the basement while we waited for Randall and Lucy to return with the hot chocolate. One by one they explained how they had been driving on the road and the blizzard had caused them to stop. Luckily Randall had just happened past and saved them. One by one.

Conversation slowly died down again and an awkward silence ensued.

"What's wrong?" Jenny asked, and I realized I was staring vacantly off into the nearest wall. It was a bad habit I had when I was thinking about something.

At that moment, I was thinking about all those cars on the road. Why hadn't we seen any of them? We'd left ours at the side of the road, but I hadn't seen any others before or after we stopped. It was possible I had missed them in the snow… But I doubted it.

I was about to ask the man sitting closest to me, named Bill, what he had done with his vehicle, but then Randall returned with Lucy and there was no opportunity. Setting my concerns aside, I decided I was being paranoid. There was probably more opportunity to get the other vehicles off the road before we arrived. There was no sense making a scene by questioning people about it.

Still, I didn't drink the hot chocolate. I didn't trust it. And neither did Jenny.

We went to bed early and a few of us slept on the floor. There were enough blankets and pillows thanks to Randall and Lucy, who offered us water and told us where the bathroom was in case we needed it.

Lying on the floor next to Jenny, I closed my eyes and drifted off to sleep, telling myself I was being paranoid. These were good people. They had helped us.

I fell into a deep slumber much quicker than usual.

But my dreams were not pleasant.

*

When I awoke it was still the middle of the night.

I heard a sound from a room nearby. A dull, rhythmic, knocking. Like someone behind a door, insisting on being let in.

Or, let OUT.

Closing my eyes, I tried desperately to ignore it. But it didn't stop for a long, long time.

*

At some point I must have fallen back asleep, because I opened my eyes to see that it was morning. The sun was shining through a small gap above the snow in the high windows above us, letting in just enough light to wake us up.

Looking around I noticed with a surreal sense of horror that we were alone.

All of the other people who had been in the basement the night prior, and who had been sleeping around us, were gone.

The woman named Barbara and her child. Bill and his family and the couple who had been sitting in the corner.

I elbowed Jenny and asked her if she saw anyone leave.

"No," she said. "I wonder what happened to them."

My heart was beating quickly in my chest and I rose to my feet, wondering what would happen if we tried the door leading back up to the main level. Would it be locked?

The burnt-bacon smell of breakfast was in the air and I realized I was starving.

"Maybe they're already awake," Jenny said. "Smells like someone's making food."

We went upstairs and found Randall was in the kitchen at the table, reading his newspaper. But nobody was cooking breakfast.

And there was no sign of the others.

"Morning, folks," Randall said, looking up from his paper. "We sure did get hit hard last night. Paper boy didn't make it, I'm afraid. This is yesterday's news!"

The old man had a smile on his face that I couldn't help but return, despite the unsettling situation.

"Thanks," I said, taking a seat. "How much did we end up getting?"

"More than six feet. And it's still coming! I can't even get the front door open."

I felt a heavy weight like cement sitting in my stomach, thinking about the fact that we were trapped in here with this man. But he was so friendly and unassuming. Not to mention, by the looks of him, he was eighty years old! Why the hell was I so suspicious of him? My gut was telling me something was wrong, and I always trusted my gut.

"What happened to everyone?" I asked, and the question came out sounding much harsher and more accusatory than I intended. I lowered my gaze when Randall looked at me with his cold blue eyes, unflinching.

"Oh, did they leave? They must have escaped before the door got blocked. Didn't even realize they were gone."

Jenny softened the mood by speaking up in a friendly voice.

"It smells good in here."

His head snapped around to look at her.

"Does it?" he asked.

"Yeah. Did you already have breakfast?"

"No."

An awkward silence hung over the three of us. It definitely smelled like someone had been cooking meat. Finally, Jenny broke the quiet by speaking up again.

"Oh. Well, if the four of us are gonna be stuck here, maybe we can work out some sort of arrangement. Do you have enough to eat, so we can make something for ourselves? We can reimburse you for the cost."

The old man smiled.

"I might have something that will satisfy you."

His grin grew even wider and he turned his gaze to look at me.

"And you? Are you hungry? Can I get you something as well?"

Despite how creepy all of this was getting, I was famished. And I had to eat something. So I nodded my head, feeling like I was making a deal with the devil for some reason.

*

After nearly an hour of waiting in the dining room, Randall finally emerged from the kitchen with a steaming tray in hand. He presented us with a plate of meat, dripping with bloody juices.

"Sorry it took so long," he said. "I had to do some butchery on these steaks. It's worth the trouble, though. You wouldn't believe how much cheaper it is when you acquire these things in bulk. I never go to the grocery store anymore. If you saw how much money I've been saving you'd see why. It's like highway robbery."

He put the steaks on plates for us, and we began to eat. There was a pool of red liquid sitting puddled in the center of my dish, looking very red and bloody, and I wondered just how undercooked the steak was going to be. I'd always been a medium sort of guy myself, pink but not bloody.

"Lucy! Breakfast!"

The old man called out.

His goddaughter came downstairs a minute later, looking surprised to see us there.

"Oh," she said, fiddling with her hair. "Are they gonna... They're staying with us?"

This struck me as odd, since she'd been there when he'd invited us to spend the night. But now she was acting clueless

122

about it. Like she was expecting us to have left like the others, despite the fact that we were snowed in.

"The door's blocked, Lucy," Randall said. "Now eat your steak."

She sat down with a moody sigh and started cutting into the piece of meat in front of her, casting awkward glances in our direction from time to time.

"You two can stay for no charge today," Randall said suddenly. "But if the snow keeps up and you're stuck in here for another night, I'll expect some payment for room and board."

Jenny looked up at me nervously, but I quickly agreed.

"That's fair. We don't have much cash on us, though. You know how it is these days, debit and credit everywhere."

"If you don't have the money, you can work off the debt. I'm always looking for help around the farm. And we've got plenty of livestock to take care of."

I nodded, thinking I had guessed right when I'd looked at the other farm buildings out back. The man definitely needed help around this huge place, and I wasn't opposed to chipping in to pay back the debt of staying and eating his food. Especially if we were gonna be stuck inside anyways.

"Sure. What did you have in mind?"

"Nothing much, just a few hours of feeding the animals, changing the hay, that sort of thing. It'll keep you busy if we keep getting more of this snow! You're gonna be getting pretty bored by tomorrow afternoon around here. No cable TV and no internet."

"How would we get out there? I thought we're snowed in?"

"There's a door in the basement that leads through a tunnel to the barns. And they're all connected. I had it built so we could get out there in case of a storm like this. Up in this area we used to get them all the time, although not so much anymore."

"Global warming," I said, nodding.

The man scowled and shook his head.

"The next ice age is coming. You'll see. Back in the seventies they said the world was gonna freeze over like it did when the Woolie Mammoths were roaming around, now they talk about global warming. It's all horseshit. The temperature goes up and down, that's all there is to it. We've got no control over it."

I knew better than to argue with the guy after he'd taken us in from the weather, and just nodded my head, thinking to myself, *The weather will clear up by tomorrow. It has to.*

*

That day passed by uneventfully and pretty soon it was dark outside again. With no WIFI and no television, there wasn't much to do around the farmhouse, but at least it was warm and there was food to go around for the four of us. Even if every meal was a very rare steak that tasted a little funny.

Jenny and I went to bed early and tried to sleep, but I could tell she was tossing and turning just as much as I was. Something about this house, and about this situation, was very wrong. Everything about it felt OFF.

Around midnight, I decided to try the door leading outside for myself, to see if it would open again. I walked over to it and opened the screen door as quietly as I could, then turned the door handle, pushing against the wood with all of my body weight. I imagined the others who had been in the basement with us doing the same thing and getting out before first light, running to their cars and gunning the engines, racing away from this place.

Maybe they'd known something was wrong with the old man too. And the more I thought about it, the more I didn't want to find out what it would be like working for him, despite my earlier promises.

The door wouldn't budge. But it didn't feel like snow blocking it on the other side. It felt like a lock. As if someone had put a deadbolt on the thing, which could only be accessed from the exterior. The bulk of the door wiggled a fraction of an inch but no further each time I pushed against it. It was like we were locked in.

Jenny was sitting upright, watching me in the darkness from where she'd been sleeping.

"What's wrong?" she asked. And I was surprised at her insight into my emotions judging just by my body language in the dark room.

"Don't freak out. I can't be sure. But, I think it's locked from the outside," I whispered, walking back over to her.

She gripped my arm with a cold hand and squeezed my bicep with her fingers digging in painfully.

"What do you mean, from the outside?"

"I'm not sure... But it doesn't feel like snow to me. Something's wrong here, can't you feel it? I'm just getting this vibe that we need to get out. Now. Tonight. Before the sun comes up and we're stuck here for another day, maybe longer."

It was hard to see much through the narrow gaps of the windows high in the room, since they were mostly covered with snow. We had no idea what it really looked like outside.

"Here, let me boost you up so you can look out the window," I said, pointing at one nearby.

We went over to it and stood below it. I put my hands out in front of me and made a step for Jenny to put her foot on.

Looking up again at the window, my heart skipped a beat.

A face was pressed up against the glass, looking in at us. Eyes that were black as night watched us, hands held up at the sides of the face to block the glare of light outside.

"Fuck," I shrieked involuntarily.

Jenny saw it too and the two of us backed away from the window, moving toward our bunks. We got in and laid back down beneath the covers, like children caught awake in the night past our bedtimes.

A second later, the face disappeared.

The whole thing was unsettling, but more than anything, it proved I was right. There was someone outside, which meant it was possible to *get outside*. The weather had improved, and the old man was keeping us trapped here as prisoners.

"We need to get out of here," I said to Jenny after we were sure the face in the window was gone.

"But how?"

As if to answer the question, a banging sound came from somewhere, just the same as it had the night before. It was a hollow, metallic sound, somehow sad and lonely in its resonance.

"What is that?" Jenny asked, gripping my hand tightly.

"I don't know," I whispered. "I heard it last night too."

CLANG, CLANG, CLANG

The noise continued, steady and rhythmic, the same pace and frequency as the night before.

With a weary glance up at the window, the two of us began to look around, hoping if we could find the source of the sound, it might somehow lead to a way out as well.

CLANG, CLANG, CLANG

It was getting louder as we got closer to the rear of the basement, and as I explored to either side I found it became softer and harder to hear.

A large mirror was set up at one end of the room we were in, and I tried to move it aside. Surprisingly, it slid to the right with ease, as if it were on a sliding set of rails.

Behind it was a weathered door, covered with flaking red paint which resembled the color of congealing blood in the darkness of the basement.

I took a glance at Jenny and she locked eyes with me. I could see she was shaking, and noticed that I was too, as I raised my hand and grabbed the door knob. Despite our fear, she nodded her head and I turned the knob, and we looked through the threshold at what lay beyond.

*

The corridor smelled like hay and manure, the familiar smells of agriculture which indicated this passageway led to a barn.

Remembering Randall's words, I decided this must be the underground tunnel which led to the other farm buildings. It stood to reason that it would lead to other exits as well.

We'd finally found our way out.

"I don't like this," Jenny said. "It feels too easy."

I hoped she was wrong about that. But I was getting a similar sensation. Especially after seeing the eyes looking in at us through the window. If they saw we were missing, they'd quickly find out where we went.

Still, what was I scared of? An old man and his daughter? I could take him if I had to, I thought to myself.

As long as he doesn't have a gun, a skeptical voice in my mind said. *Or he could have help. You saw the face in the window, and it didn't look like him. And you said for yourself there had to be more people working on this farm.*

I was more and more scared with each step we took down the long tunnel, and I noticed it was getting colder as well.

Finally we emerged into a dimly lit barn. The two of us ducked down behind a wall and watched around the corner as a worker entered the large space.

Hay was all over the floor and I assumed this was an area which contained animals - thus explaining the hay and manure. The man was carrying what looked like a bag of feed, and he dumped it into a trough at the center of the large space.

"Alright," he called out, removing a pistol from a holster attached to his belt. "Dinner time, piggies!"

People began to emerge from the cages and pens I'd presumed were meant for farm animals. Instead of cows and pigs, men and women emerged from each one. They were teary-eyed and some were weeping.

As they got down on their hands and knees to eat the slop they'd been given, I noticed something even more horrifying.

The people were missing pieces of themselves. Arms and legs, and various other parts had been shaved off of them, the wounds half-healed in some cases and covered with bloody bandages.

"Oh my God..." Jenny whispered from beside me, gripping my arm tightly. She was seeing the same thing I was.

The old man's words came back to me, from when we had been sitting around his breakfast table.

Sorry it took so long... I had to do some butchery on these steaks...

You wouldn't believe how much cheaper it is when you acquire these things in bulk...

I never go to the grocery store anymore. If you saw how much money I've been saving you'd see why...

It's like highway robbery...

The whole time he'd been laughing about it in our faces. He was collecting people at the side of the road…

And eating them.

Maybe he was in some sort of twisted cult or secret society. I'd heard rumors of such people existing. Online forums where cannibalism was discussed in great detail. I'd even heard there was a name for it - Zambian Meat.

I began to gag as the realization settled in, and I thought about the implications.

"Jenny…. The steaks…"

She covered her mouth with her hand, trembling as she whispered back to me.

"Jesus. He fed us fucking *people*, Jason."

I couldn't help it, I threw up involuntarily, and Jenny did as well, just as the worker was leaving the barn, going out through a door which looked to lead outside.

After several moments of retching and coughing up bile as quietly as we could, we gathered our wits again.

"There," I said, pointing at the exit. "That's gotta be the way out. Come on, let's go. We'll get the police and come back for these people."

The two of us took one last look around the barn for any signs of guards and began to run towards the exit.

Instantly, I realized our mistake.

The people there were so desperate to get out, so afraid of the situation they were in, that as soon as they saw us, they began to scream for help.

"We're saved!" a woman yelled.

"Jason, Jenny!" Bill, the man from the night prior, was seen at the trough. He was now missing a leg and hobbled over to us, falling to the ground hard at one point and then crawling, grasping the straw-covered floor with his hands as he dragged himself the rest of the way on his belly.

Before I knew it, the man was holding onto my leg, weeping like a child.

"You have to get us out. You have to help us!" he screamed, over and over again.

There were thick chains attached to ankle bracelets that held each one of them, preventing them from escaping the barn. But they didn't think about that detail as they wailed and cried, begging us to let them out, to take them with us.

"We're going to get help! You have to let us go!" I tried to reason with them, but they were no longer thinking properly.

"The hot chocolate!" Bill was yelling now. "Don't drink the hot chocolate!"

Footsteps could be heard outside and Jenny and I quickly realized the worker was returning. My heart jackhammering in my chest, I kicked my leg out of Bill's grasp. He scrambled after us as we raced out of the room, heading for the door which I assumed led into another barn beside this one.

A second after we left the barn, I heard the door open and the worker was in the doorway, yelling, "Shut up and eat your slop! We ain't lettin' you outta here so quit asking!"

He was quiet suddenly and I wondered if he sensed something was off. The group of prisoners were still making a lot of noise, asking to be let go, talking to us even though we were no longer in the room. I wondered how long a few of them had been kept here, and if they had gone completely mad by this point.

CLANG, CLANG, CLANG

The sound we'd been hearing from the basement was much louder now, and I looked around at the new space we were in, seeing it was not a barn, but a butcher room. Blood stains were on the floor and spattered the walls. There were drains at the center of the area and the smooth floors sloped toward them, to funnel blood away from stainless steel tables where the gruesome work was done. Hair and pieces of bone and flesh were lying on the ground in places, but the tables had been meticulously cleaned and polished.

Giant chest freezers and refrigerators were arranged along one wall. Hooks were hanging from the ceiling on a conveyor belt which brought carcasses to and from another room. It was quite cold in here, I noticed, and when I breathed out I could see a puff of fog escaping my lungs.

CLANG, CLANG, CLANG

The sound came again, and this time it was from one specific fridge, which I noticed was rattling back and forth each time the noise was made.

Despite my fear and desire to escape, I found myself drawn to the fridge. On wobbly legs I wandered to it and stood in front of it, breathing deeply and taking in the coppery-smelling air.

"We need to get out of here," Jenny said urgently. But I knew it was pointless. There was no other way out.

My entire body was trembling as I gripped the fridge door handle and prepared myself for what was inside.

I opened it and felt my skin turn ice cold.

The man inside the fridge was still alive, but just barely. His skin was turning blue. His lips were chapped, broken, and frost-covered. His arms and legs had been removed, the stumps cauterized with a hot brand.

He opened his mouth to scream and I saw he had no tongue. All he could do to call for help was what he had been doing.

With as much force as he could muster, he banged his head hard against the inside of the fridge, hitting his forehead where a black, swollen bruise had developed.

CLANG, CLANG, CLANG!

And then he mouthed the words which I could easily make out, despite the fact that I didn't know how to read lips.

There were only two of them, and they were plain enough to see, and easy enough to guess considering the situation.

"Kill me," the man in the fridge said without sound.

And then the door crashed in behind us.

The worker entered the room and we were still hidden behind a large cabinet, but just barely.

There was only one place to go. Only one place to hide.

My girlfriend and I crammed ourselves into the refrigerator, taking up residence with the man inside, and I pulled the door closed, hoping no one had seen us enter.

We held our collective breath, and even the man in there with us did the same, as if hoping maybe with our help he could still be free of this place.

It was freezing cold inside the fridge. Unbearable. My skin began to feel as if it were being stabbed with pins and needles as I tried to adjust my body weight to get more comfortable. But it was impossible.

There wasn't an inch of extra room. It felt like I couldn't breath, as if I were suffocating, as if my lungs were turning into ice.

And then footsteps could be heard from just outside, and I dared not move an inch.

Raspy breathing sounds, and then a cough echoed, and then the door opened and I saw Randall outside with the worker who had been looking for us. Lucy was with them, and all three had pistols and shotguns pointed in our direction. If we moved an inch, I had no doubt they would use them. These people would not hesitate to kill us.

The old man held a large caliber pistol in one hand, and in the other he had a cigarillo. He put it to his lips and took a puff, smiling at us. Then he breathed out a frosty plume of smoke and began to laugh.

"You know, I offered the two of you a job for a reason. You looked like hard workers."

He let out a sigh.

"But if you'd prefer to be meat… Well, we can make that happen too. We're always in need. After all, Mitchell's Zambian Meat goes out all over the world. We're a very popular supplier in our niche demographic. And we always need more inventory."

I tried to protest, to tell him we'd do what he asked, we'd do anything, but all I could do was chatter my teeth as I tried to form a sentence.

A second later the door was closed and we were left in darkness again. In the cold. Unable to move, just like if we'd gone into a ditch during that storm and been buried in the snow.

Nobody will find you until the Spring. And by then, they'll need dental records to identify you.

I was starting to think we would have been better off in the ditch, when another one of Randall's workers surprised us by opening the fridge door again an hour later. We could barely move by that point, our fingers and toes numb with frostbite, but we managed to crawl out onto the floor.

After warming up enough to speak, I thanked the man, but he didn't answer. When he opened his mouth, I saw he had no tongue.

He simply motioned to the door, and to the exit, and watched passively as we escaped into the frozen winter air, running for miles in our bare feet until we found a town far away from that house. I didn't trust anyone living nearby.

I didn't trust anyone ever again.

All I can see now when I look at other people, even Jenny, is Randall Mitchell, sitting at that dining room table cutting up a bloody steak and putting pieces of it in his mouth.

It's like highway robbery…

Imposter Syndrome

I kept having the same nightmare, over and over again. All I could remember was bits and pieces.

Looking in the misted mirror of the bathroom, I saw my reflection. Then I noticed it.

Blood begins to pour from a wound in the side of my neck which seems to grow and spread in a cracking web like a windshield smashed with a rock. It gets bigger and chunks of flesh crumble and slough off of me like ruined plaster from an ancient building's facade. As if I am a porcelain doll which has begun to age and chip and flake away with time, revealing the darkness beneath.

But it gets worse. There is something within that festering wound-bed and I turn my head to look and see eyes staring back at me from within it. Looking back at me, familiar as my own reflection.

There is more, but I can never remember it. There has to be more.

*

It all started a while back when I had my first novel published. All the trouble, it began with a good thing.

I write horror as a part time job, but I only started doing that recently. A little over a year ago I managed to put together about fifty thousand words concerning a security guard who gets caught up in a murder investigation in an old haunted asylum where he works. It was partially inspired by a job I had about a decade ago working as a security guard in a century and a half old asylum in my hometown. The sanatorium where the novel was set has been the source of real-life rumors and legends for years in the city where I live.

Even after all this time I still get nightmares about the place, so it was easy enough to write a horror novel about it. I showed it to some friends and one of them had a connection in the publishing industry. After a meeting we made an agreement to have a thousand copies printed and I received a tidy advance for my efforts. But the bigger joy was finally being able to declare myself a "published author."

I was thrilled! It was a dream come true. I had wanted to be an author for as long as I could remember. I had attempted to write a novel before but had failed miserably the first time - this felt like redemption! I felt like I'd made a big accomplishment and I wanted to share the news with people.

So I posted about the upcoming publication on Reddit. I'd written the novel piecemeal and posted most of it to nosleep as a series so it seemed appropriate to share the news with the community.

I was amazed how many people commented to congratulate me and cheer me on.

Then someone in the comments very kindly asked for advice. They congratulated me and asked what recommendations I could offer them as an aspiring writer who wants to be published one day.

What did I know? I asked myself. I had just written this series and happened to have a connection to a publisher. If not for that it probably wouldn't have even happened for me. It felt like I was pretending, like I was just faking and acting like I was a real writer.

That was when it hit me.

Imposter syndrome like I had never felt it before.

Sure, I'd had that feeling in the past. Maybe we all have. That overwhelming urge to climb right out of your own skin. Because who people think you are isn't you. You've wanted to be something special, sure. But you're not. I'm not.

I wasn't really a writer. I was just…

An imposter.

My writing wasn't even all that good compared to others. I would never see my name on the New York Times Bestsellers list. I would be lucky to find a few family members willing to buy the book.

I logged off after leaving a brief reply, trying my best to give advice when I felt like I didn't have the right to do so. I felt like a phony, a hack.

I went to bed early and had a night of fitful dreams and existential nightmares.

In my dream I was standing in front of my bathroom mirror. It was so vivid I could feel the cold tile floor beneath my bare feet. Mist hung in the air from the shower and water clung to my skin in fat droplets as I looked at my reflection.

It was fogged up so I wiped the mirror dry with a towel and saw something odd. My skin was peeling and cracking on the right side of my neck and face, like an old sunburn ready to come off. It was red and angry-looking around the blistering wound.

I peeled away the thin layer of dead skin at the center of it and brushed my fingers against something. Then reflexively pulled my hand away, horrified at what I felt there.

There was something round underneath the dead skin. Something large, slick, and warm, moving around.

I tried to scream but no sound came out of me as something like a giant black bubble began to emerge from my neck and the side of my face. A large, ovaloid shape, covered in sticky, stretching strands of goo. It seemed to have a mind of its own as it wriggled and squirmed to free itself like an ectopic twin gaining self awareness and attempting independence. It defied all logic and physics, biology and common sense, as it pulled itself out from its hidden place, prying its way out from inside of me.

There was a strange sense of losing something, as if a part of me were going with it as it separated from me.

As it emerged fully I saw it was another person. A doppelganger. An exact duplicate version of me covered in greenish yellow goo which dripped and globbed onto the tile bathroom floor.

Suddenly the doppelganger turned to look at me. He pulled the last part of his soggy, sticky foot from the hidden space where he had been residing inside of me and gave me a good look up and down, as if appraising me. Then he smiled, his teeth perfectly white and unblemished.

"Back to sleep," he said, and as he did I felt my eyelids begin to grow heavy, and my vision went dark. "Big day tomorrow."

*

The next morning I woke up in my own bed, feeling like it had all surely been a terrible dream, and not even able to remember most of it.

My phone's alarm was singing its familiar song, telling me it was 6 AM and time to get up and get ready for work. It was still dark outside now, in late November, and I felt like I had barely slept. My wife was snoring, sprawled out in bed and instantly taking up my body-space. I got up reluctantly, feeling a pang of jealousy while I watched her resume her slumber in the darkness.

I had a bad headache on the right side of my head, from my temple down to my jaw. This was a terrible sign for so early in the day. It meant I would likely wind up with a migraine by the afternoon and would be in bed early by 7PM trying to sleep it off. Vaguely I remembered my dream and there being a pain on that side of my head, some sort of injury, perhaps. I wondered if the headache had plagued my sleep with nightmares.

Stumbling from the bedroom in the dark I closed the door behind me and went into the bathroom to brush my teeth and get ready for work. Due to my throbbing temples and pressure-filled eyeballs, I refused to turn the light on for as long as possible. But eventually I relented so I could get in the shower - I didn't want to attempt that in the dark.

Strangely, I saw the bathtub was wet as was the towel, as if someone had recently showered. But Christine had been asleep. Odd. And the floor was wet too.

The nightmare flashed through my mind again in pieces but I didn't remember it all right away. Just standing in front of the mirror and peeling something from my skin. That was all I could remember as I turned the knobs and water began to blast from the rusty showerhead. But I struggled desperately to remember the rest of the dream. It seemed important somehow.

I finished getting ready for work in the darkened apartment, not wanting to wake my wife by turning on too many lights. There was a strange feeling of someone watching me, and the cats were hiding somewhere instead of coming out for their breakfast when they heard the sounds of me getting ready as they usually did.

The elevator was slow to arrive so I stood waiting with my work bag in hand, looking at my phone with my other hand. It was still early, and I'd make it to work in plenty of time as long as I didn't get delayed by traffic.

When I got downstairs, I ambled out to the parking lot in the pre-dawn light. They say it's always darkest before dawn, and it's true. As someone who has worked plenty of night shifts outdoors, I can attest to that. It was nearly pitch-black outside, since everyone in the building was still sleeping and our security light had burned out a few days prior.

As I walked across the rain-dampened parking lot towards my car, I hit the unlock button on the key fob. The front lights of the car blinked on, momentarily illuminating the darkened area around the vehicle.

That was when I saw him.

He was standing in the shadows about twenty feet away from my car, wearing what looked like a trench coat. His hands were in his pockets and he was just standing there in the parking lot, in the dark, watching me. Staring at me.

I froze for a second, my breath catching and my chest hitching with fear.

"Hello?" I said, unsure.

"Hello?" he called back, his voice a completely accurate imitation of mine.

"Ha ha," I laughed nervously.

"Ha ha," he entoned back.

I became nervous and quickly walked towards my car, which meant moving closer to him. He suddenly began to mimic my footsteps, walking in time with me, his path taking him towards my car as well.

Noticing that, I stopped.

"What are you doing?"

"What are you doing?"

"This isn't funny, you need to stop. I need to go to work."

"This isn't funny, you need to stop. I need to go to work."

He repeated back everything I said, obnoxious as a little kid. But it wasn't annoying, it was terrifying. Especially in the darkness of the parking lot where I couldn't see his face. And even more so as the details of my dream began to come back to me, bit by bit.

"What do you want?" I asked him.

For once he didn't mimic me. He simply stepped forward, his face suddenly illuminated in the dull glow of light coming from inside.

His face was my own. An exact replica of mine.

He just smiled, his teeth bright white like they had never eaten a meal, never drank coffee or been stained red with wine. He smiled wide and shook his head, as if saying no. He wouldn't tell me what he wanted. That would be too easy.

"You'll find out soon enough."

The man from my dream who looked just like me turned away and began to walk back into the shadows, disappearing from sight. Before I knew it, he was gone.

I got into my car, feeling frightened and shaky. What did he want? And was it really the creature from my dream? Or was it just some creep who happened to look like me? Just the world's worst and strangest coincidence?

No part of me believed that last option. I was certain this was something supernatural. Whoever that was - he had been a part of me. And we had parted ways from each other the night before.

When I got to work, I ran through all the possibilities of what could be happening to me. A mental break didn't seem completely out of the question, but it also occurred to me that this could be an unexplained phenomena - something that had never happened before.

Maybe this was something that had not happened for many hundreds of years. Maybe it was a once in millenia event. But there could be a record of it somewhere.

Doppelgangers - I knew that term. And that was what this seemed to be. A doppelganger. So when I got to work, I looked up what those were.

I found that it was a subject which had been discussed over many centuries in recent history.

One account in particular caught my eye. The case of Vice Admiral Sir George Tryon. On June 22nd 1893, he was seen by several guests at a party being thrown by his wife at their family home in Eaton Square, London. The only problem was, he was off the coast of Syria at that moment, going down with his ship - the HMS Victoria.

Another case - John Donne, an English poet, was said to have seen his wife carrying their dead child in her arms, walking through the room twice and then disappearing before his eyes on the same night as the stillbirth of their daughter.

The long and short of it was, based on these stories, Doppelgangers were a bad omen. They were a sign of death.

No wonder he hadn't wanted to tell me what he wanted. He wanted to kill me. Or perhaps to tell me I was dying.

I tried to focus on my work for the rest of the day but it was difficult to get much done with such dark thoughts in my mind. Finally, my lunch break rolled around and I went down to the cafeteria and scrolled Reddit on my phone while drinking coffee and eating.

There were a bunch of notifications when I logged on, all comments and awards for a story that I didn't remember posting. But then when I read it, I vaguely remembered it. Only I had never written the story - it had just been in my head.

Weirdly, someone was also answering comments from my account as well. And I knew immediately who it was. The doppelganger. The sonofabitch was trying to usurp my username. And he was using my ideas!

The worst part was, it was far better written than anything I had done before.

My phone rang suddenly and I answered it at my desk, whispering into the receiver.

"Hello?"

"It's me," said the doppelganger.

"What the hell, man!? You stole my idea! I was gonna write the story!"

"Ha! You would have just screwed it up. Admit it. That's why you've been thinking about writing it for so long but never got around to it."

I didn't respond. He was right.

"What the hell do you want, anyways?"

He laughed for a few long moments before answering.

"Your life. You admitted it to yourself. You're not good enough. Just give it up. I'll take over from here."

"Who are you?"

"The real you. You're just an imposter, remember? You wished you could crawl out of your own skin, well, now you have. All you have to do is slink away like you do best. Don't want to get into another fight with your wife? Don't worry, I'll take care of it for you. When you get home she'll have it all out of her system. And then tomorrow you can take the day off work. I'll fill in for you, how does that sound?"

"No... I've seen this movie before, and it didn't turn out well for Michael Keaton. Just go back to hell or wherever you came from, you freak."

I slammed the phone down, startling my coworkers sitting nearby. Smiling awkwardly at them, I tried to look normal and went back to work. But it was difficult. There was another me out there - and he was trying to become my full-time replacement. Not only that, but he might want me dead to more easily fulfill that goal.

When I got home that night I found my key didn't work in the door. I knocked and my wife Christine answered.

"Oh, you're back! Did you get the... Where's the wine? I thought that's what you were going out for?"

There were candles lit on the table and a nice dinner had been prepared. I realized immediately who had done it all. The doppelganger.

"Forget it, we don't need the wine!" she said. "I'm just so happy you finally did something romantic for me like this! You never do stuff like this," she looked excited but at the same time hurt, as if not able to understand why it took me so long to do something like this. I couldn't understand it myself.

It had taken another me - a better me - to do what I couldn't. I wanted to disappear, to shrink out of sight and become an invisible speck of dust in that moment - to do exactly what the doppelganger wanted. I didn't deserve her, and she was a saint to put up with me. But that was a cliche - really I just needed to do better.

"I'm going to start doing things like this more often," I said. "I promise."

She looked doubtful, but with a glimmer of hope in her eyes that said she would try to believe me.

*

Later that night I woke up from sleeping, needing to go to the bathroom. Yeah, I know, I'm getting old.

When I came back into the darkened bedroom, I saw him standing there, in the shadows.

My wife was fast asleep and he stood at the foot of the bed, staring at me, just his silhouette, black as the reaper's shadow. He raised a finger to his lips - quiet.

"Why are you here," I whispered. "Just leave us alone. No one asked you to come here."

He stood over the bed, looking at me, saying nothing.

"Your kind - doppelganger, fetch, whatever you're called - your kind comes when someone's dying, right? Well, there's nobody dying here. So leave. Just go."

I realized I was trying to negotiate with something I didn't understand, but that didn't stop me. He wasn't budging, but I wasn't going to give up that easily. Despite my worst fears standing in front of me, I screamed at him, desperate for him to be gone. Desperate to be the only ME again.

"What are you still standing there for? Didn't you hear me? Just leave! LEAVE! LEAVE! LEAVE!!!"

Christine was turning on her bedside lamp and blinking her eyes as I continued to scream. She stood up and ran over to me and I realized there was no one else in the bedroom but us.

We were alone again.

"Who are you yelling at?" she asked, looking worried.

I didn't know how to tell her the truth. I still don't.

After telling her I was sleepwalking and having some sort of terrible nightmare, she went back to bed. I'm still awake. I can't sleep, knowing he could still be out there. When I wake up tomorrow, what else will he have taken from me?

I'll have to fight for my life if I want to keep it.

But for once, that doesn't sound so bad.

A World Without Fire

A cold wind was blowing, rustling the canvas of our tent violently in its gale and sending freezing spikes of air into our skin. My wife and I were huddled together for warmth, shivering and chattering our teeth. The blankets were never thick enough anymore, and each night seemed to grow colder than the one before.

My stomach rumbled with hunger again, and I felt a sharp stab of pain in my gut at the same time - my body revolting against the spoiled meat and rotten vegetation I'd been forced to eat the day prior. Food was scarce this time of year, and we'd been desperate that day.

Ever since fire became a thing of the past, we'd all been struggling to survive. Struggling to stay warm. Those who were left of us, anyways.

The camp where we lived was home to nearly fifty people, and each winter we lost more. As much as we might have wanted to, no one dared to have children, since we were all terrified of their noisy cries attracting the things which came in the night. The hungry creatures that came with the darkness.

When humans lost the ability to make fire, there were other changes too. It was like a celestial shift had happened, and we had moved into a new era - one in which man was no longer in charge. Instead, ancient things which we had no name for emerged from the depths of the deepest and darkest caves, and began to quickly take over, and to devour the weak and the helpless. People disappeared in the night, never to be seen again, and we knew the monsters had taken them.

But none of us have been able to capture or kill a single one of them. They are elusive as ghosts, and quick as vipers.

It wasn't only fire that went away when the great change happened. We might have been able to maintain civilization if that were the case. But we didn't just lose the ability to make a flame. Everything that cast a light or made a spark ceased to function. All electronics and every computer on the planet went out at once, like someone had put their finger on a giant light switch and pushed it down, plunging the entire world into permanent darkness, and back into the technological dark ages.

We all thought that early man was simple and stupid, for not understanding how to make fire. But none of us considered the possibility that fire was not something earned, but something given.

Fire was a gift from the gods. And we angered the hell out of them.

We ravaged nature. We killed off most species of animals. We turned the oceans into cesspools of plastic and oil. And we destroyed this once great planet we'd been given.

So the gods decided to take back the sacred gift they had granted us so long ago, as punishment for how we had used it. They took away the spark and the fire that we had harnessed for our own purposes, and they left us cold and in darkness once again, just like we had been once before, so long ago.

"Honey, are you awake?" I asked my wife in a soft voice.

"Yeah," she answered back immediately. "I can't sleep. It's too quiet."

That was the other strange thing about the world now. Without cars and electricity it was always quiet. It was silent everywhere all the time - the only noise was the sound of your own breathing. It was rare to encounter animals anymore. They were so skittish and terrified since the change happened. And who could blame them?

We called them shadows, the creatures that came from the darkness, because that was what they looked like. You just saw a dark outline of something moving towards you, and by then it was too late. You were already dead.

They were impossibly quiet. Insatiable in their hunger.

As I was thinking about the creatures, I heard something from just outside. The sound of breathing and movement. Gooseflesh rose across my skin and the hair stood up on the back of my neck. My wife grabbed my hand and gripped it tightly in hers.

The two of us held our collective breath and waited to be disemboweled. If it happened, it would happen in an instant.

Another rustling sound of movement, and a heavy breathing sound.

Whatever it was, it was very close.

"I'm telling you, that's what he said…"

"Fire, though? Fire doesn't exist anymore."

I sighed with relief, and my wife did the same, releasing her vice-like grip on my hand. People were talking outside our tent and the two of us both sat upright, hearing the excited chatter back and forth. At least we weren't going to die. That was always a relief.

"How can he be sure? He's never even seen it before. He's just a kid…"

"I know, but he sounded positive. I'm going to tell Gregory, and we'll see what he says."

My wife, Sarah, and I got up and went outside, eager to find out what was going on. Lisa and Cathy were heading towards the larger tent belonging to the camp's leader, Gregory.

"What's going on?" I asked Lisa.

The two women looked back and forth at each other nervously.

"Jason said he found something while he was out exploring. There's a laboratory just outside the city, about eight miles from here. He said…"

She'd stopped talking and was looking uncertain now.

"What? What did he find?"

"Fire," she said. "Jason told me he found fire."

"Impossible," my wife whispered, her eyes wide. A tear rolled down one cheek. "That's impossible."

*

"I doubt very much that what your boy says is true," Gregory said piously.

We were inside the elder's large round tent. The outside was encircled with a ring of furniture and at the center was a large chair - almost a throne but not quite. Nearby, on a small sofa, sat Gregory's three wives, looking on passively and listening to the conversation. They rarely spoke, especially in public.

"Why would he lie?" Lisa asked. "He wouldn't make up something like that. He knows how important it is."

"How did he describe it exactly? The boy has never even seen fire. It was gone before he was born."

"He described it exactly! Warm, orange and red with spiked tips. He said it shimmered and heated his hands when he held them close."

Gregory looked unconvinced. He put his chin in his hand contemplatively and sighed.

"I will not risk a search party based on a story from a child. Our best people have worked to make fire for years. I doubt very much that a small boy managed to find it in one afternoon of hiking. What exactly was he doing eight miles away from the camp? He knows better than to be venturing that far on his own."

"He was trying to help! He likes to explore. And the shadows don't come out during the day.   The boy can run fast and he always gets back before dark."

"Until one day he doesn't. What if there is heavy snow? Or if he trips and sprains his ankle? You should know better than to let the boy go so far alone. And I will not permit him to do something so reckless again!"

"It isn't up to you! I'm his mother."

"And I am the leader of this camp! I'll hear no more of this tonight. We will discuss it further after the sun rises. The shadows are never far off. We cannot risk a discussion like this now."

That seemed to settle the argument. Everyone nodded and filed out of the tent quietly, going back to their sleeping quarters. Except for Lisa who followed Sarah and I back to our own enclosure.

We let her inside, and a little while later Cathy came with their son, Jason - the boy who claimed he had found fire. Within a minute of their arrival, they were telling us what they wanted to do.

"Gregory will never allow it. That's why we need you to go. You're the only one who can keep up with him. I've tried. The boy is way too fast. And I have a bad knee, I'd never make it back by sunset."

I had once been a runner, but that was a long time ago, I tried to explain. I was out of shape.

"Oh, c'mon," said Cathy. "I've seen you out there. Remember when we got lost that one time and the creatures came after us? You saved us all by carrying Jason on your shoulders, when he was younger. You're just being modest."

"That was a long time ago..." I said, but I was already convinced. I would go with the boy to see what he had found.

Still, I was terrified. I didn't want to go for the same reasons Gregory had mentioned. Even if he was being overly cautious, he was right. We could encounter a snow storm, or wolves, one of us could get injured, or worse. There were a thousand ways to die out there these days. Not the least of which was a run-in with another group of people. You never knew what to expect when you encountered another group.

It must have shown in my eyes, because Sarah grabbed my hand and gripped it tightly.

"You don't have to go if you don't want to."

What she didn't say, but didn't need to, was that she wanted me to go. Winter was knocking at the front gate and pretty soon it wouldn't wait another minute to be let inside. And I could already tell it was going to be a cold one.

"How far did he say it was?"

"Remember Highway Five?" she asked.

It took me a few moments, but eventually I remembered and nodded.

"Just past that, down the next road to the right. About eight miles each way."

That was no short run. But if the weather stayed clear and we didn't get any snow it wouldn't be a problem. The two of us would have to set out at first light, though. And we would need to keep a steady pace.

"Alright. But try to break the news to Gregory gently. I don't want this to look like we're trying to ignore his instructions."

"Except we are."

"Yeah. But try not to make it sound like that."

*

I set off with Jason right after the sun came up and the two of us began to jog immediately. The boy was ten years old but he could sprint like an Olympic runner. Pretty soon I was having trouble keeping up with him.

"Hey, slow down," I called after him, wheezing. "We need to conserve our energy."

"I'm fine," he yelled back. "Take your time. You can catch up with me."

Before long he was far off ahead of me, and I had a stitch growing in my side that felt like a knife blade digging between my ribs.

I sat down on the road and tried to catch my breath, and looked to see Jason was long gone.

The blue skies had turned gray and I looked up to see flurries drifting down from above. The first snowfall of the season, and it had chosen today of all days to arrive.

Standing up from where I was sitting at the side of the road, I began to jog again. I just hoped that Jason would know better than to leave the road, and would keep going in a straight line until I caught up with him.

After a half hour of jogging at a steady pace I saw him. He was sitting on the hood of an abandoned car which had been left at the side of the road. The gasoline-powered vehicles had stopped working at the same time as everything else. I remembered at the time everyone thought it was a large-scale EMP from a foreign military, meant to cast the western world back into the dark ages. But then the connection was made with the lack of fire, and everyone understood, it was something far worse than that. And it affected everyone. Not just us. The whole planet had gone dark all at once.

"I thought you were a runner," Jason said, looking impatient. He jumped up from the car hood and looked ready to start going again.

"We should go back," I said, panting. "It's snowing. We can't risk it if it starts to really come down."

"Oh, c'mon! It never really piles up the first snowfall of the year. It'll all be melted by noon. Let's keep going. What if the fire stops working? There might only be so much of it."

He had a point there. If a lightning strike or a chemical fire had caused this freak event to occur it would be short-lived. We would be lucky to find a few embers still smoking.

Suddenly I felt hopeful again. I could imagine a fire and the glowing warmth it would give off, and I smiled.

"Okay. But if it turns into a blizzard we go back right away. Just… Hang on… Let me rest for a minute."

After a few minutes I stood up again and started to move at a slow jog. Jason matched my pace but then quickly began to run, loping up ahead of me and disappearing over a hill, leaving me behind.

By noon the two of us reached the lab.

We went inside and I looked over my shoulder to see the snow was beginning to accumulate on the grass, although the roads were still clear. Hopefully they would stay that way.

"Okay, show me where you saw the fire," I told Jason.

He was eager to show me his discovery. My stomach had butterflies in it, and I realized I was actually hopeful. My ears listened closely for the sound of a Bunson burner left on or the soft hiss of some gas-powered flame. I sniffed the air for the burnt smell of charcoal and smoke that had been absent for so many years.

I could imagine the warmth of it, last felt so long ago. I imagined food being cooked, meat that was charred and delicious, instead of raw, rancid, and spoiled.

"In here," Jason yelled over his shoulder, leading me deeper into the lab.

It was dark in here, and the chances of running into the shadow creatures was much more likely in a place like this. They would sometimes hide out in darkened buildings to get away from the sun during the day.

"Stay close," I called to Jason. "I told your mom I'd keep an eye on you, remember?"

"Come on," he yelled back to me. "It's right in here."

I followed him into a large laboratory with beakers and tabletop centrifuges, various instruments and jugs of chemicals. Everything was sterile and white, as if this place had been abandoned during a regular work day and no one had ever returned.

My stomach felt like there was a cinder block inside as Jason led me to a tall metal tank that looked like an oversized oxygen cylinder and pointed at it excitedly.

"Look!" he shouted, pointing at it. "Fire! See! I told you!"

I stood staring in wide-eyed dismay at the gas tank.

On the side of it was the old symbol we had all used so many years ago. The symbol for flammable - an orange-red flame with pointed tips painted on the canister.

"What?" Jason asked. "It's fire, isn't it? Feel it. It's warm."

The sun was shining through a nearby window, the heat from the beam of light landing on the side of the gas chemical tank. I wasn't sure what was inside of it exactly, but I noticed there was a slight shimmer above it, like above the asphalt of a road on a very hot day. Maybe it was leaking something? Maybe the combination of air with the chemical inside was causing a reaction that produced heat?

I stood up and walked over to the tank, touching the side of it and feeling that it was quite warm, perhaps just heated by the sun through the window at my back, or perhaps by something else, it was difficult to tell.

Letting out a sigh, I turned to look at Jason, and tried to think of how to explain this without letting him down too badly. I could tell that he had been excited too. He had wanted to be a hero for the camp, and now he would feel like a fool.

I didn't want that for him.

"You did well, Jason. This is a gas tank - they used to use these to store oxygen and propane, which you could make fire with. I'm not sure what's inside, but it feels warm to the touch - and that's great. It might help us through the winter somehow, if we can use it to our advantage. But this isn't fire. I'm sorry. What you see here is the symbol for fire - maybe someone drew it for you once and that's why you recognized it. This meant that whatever was in this tank could be set ablaze. It was a warning, so people didn't get injured. Does that make sense?"

I could see the distrust in his eyes, a sign of how much hope he'd had in this endeavor.

"Are you sure? My mom said that's what fire looks like. She drew a picture that looked just like that."

"I'm sure she did. But I saw real fire many times, back in the old days, and this isn't it. If your mom were here right now she would say the same thing, trust me."

He lowered his head and looked at the ground. Turning around, he began to shuffle towards the exit.

"Come on, let's go. I don't wanna be here one minute longer," he said, sounding upset.

"Hang on," I called after him. "I'm gonna bring this with us. It could help keep us warm through the winter. If there's more of this stuff, it might really help us out. We could even use it to cook food, if our science people can get it hot enough. Maybe they can even use it to make fire again!"

"You really think so?" he asked, running back over to help.

"Yeah, I do. Come on, help me lift it up. It's heavy, be careful."

*

Jason and I left the laboratory to find the road covered in a fine layer of powder. More snow was drifting down from above now, creating a haze which was difficult to see through. And it was colder outside than it had been all year. I cinched my coat tighter around my neck and pulled my gloves out from my pockets, putting them on.

The warmth of the gas tank was already beginning to dissipate and I felt my hopes fading with it. But I tried not to let that show to Jason, who had a half-hopeful smile on his face.

"Wow, it's really coming down," he said, looking around in wonderment. "How much longer do you think we have until sundown?"

"A few hours at least. But it will come on fast with these clouds. Let's start jogging. You can go ahead if you want, you don't need to wait for me. This tank is gonna slow me down some."

What I didn't say to him was that I was going to ditch the tank at the first opportunity if I was worried about making it back before sunset. I wasn't going to risk my life on the off-chance that it would amount to something. And we could always go back for it the following day.

Jason didn't want to leave me, though. He kept up with my slow jogging pace for a couple hours until I stopped to rest. The sun was getting close to the horizon by that point and I was a little worried about our progress. It was much slower going with the snow piling up on the road. Both of us had almost fallen on several occasions, and potholes and ruts were now obscured by the fine powder, making running much scarier than before. I'd already turned my ankle once and was limping slightly. I could feel my shoe getting tighter around my swelling foot.

"You okay?" Jason asked nervously. "I can carry the tank for a while."

I shook my head. It wasn't that I couldn't use his help. The problem was that the tank was totally cold now. I was sure that the warmth we'd both felt was just the heat from the sun through the window glass, causing the tank to grow hot throughout the day in the lab. Now that we had been outside in the snow for a while it was freezing cold, even through my gloves.

"I'll be alright," I said. "You start running ahead. That's an order. Not a request. I want you to go back and tell everyone what we found, but I don't want you stranded out here with me if I have to hide somewhere for the night."

I stood up and started walking again, my hurt ankle feeling twice as bad as before, now that I'd given it a chance to rest. Each step made me wince with agony.

Jason didn't argue, at least. He knew that if I was ordering him to do something it was serious.

He nodded with a grave look on his face and took off down the road, running quickly, and disappearing into the snowy mist in the distance.

*

With Jason gone I set the tank of gas in a ditch at the side of the road and covered it superficially with snow. There was still a chance it would be useful in some way, so I figured I would come back for it the following day. But I wasn't going to risk carrying it any longer.

I began to jog, then picked up my pace and began to run. Every time my left foot hit the pavement a lightning bolt of pain shot up my leg, but I ignored it as best as I could.

Looking up, I could no longer see the position of the sun. The cloud cover overhead was so thick that it felt like it was getting dark already, despite the fact that it was still mid-afternoon.

I couldn't help but wonder if the shadow-things would come out early if it stayed dark like this. The clouds overhead were dumping snow down on me in heavy globs that soaked through my coat and my gloves, freezing my hands.

Before long, the snow was up to my shins. My legs were exhausted from running and felt like JELLO. My ankle was a throbbing, swollen ball of pain, screaming at me to stop.

And finally I did.

By that point I had no idea what time it was anymore. All I knew was that I would not make it back before dusk. I had to find a place to camp out for the night. And it would be a very cold, very terrifying night, if I even managed to find such a place.

Looking around, I saw an old gas station down the road. It was my best bet, I thought. If I could make it there.

Ignoring my exhaustion and the horrible agony of my ankle, I picked myself up and started running again.

About thirty paces in, I stepped on the edge of a pothole, and turned my bad ankle again, much worse this time. I felt something tear and a horrible pain ripped through the side of my foot and halfway up my lower leg.

This time I couldn't walk on it. I had to hop and hobble along on one leg, struggling desperately to make the remaining distance to the gas station before darkness fell completely.

When I got there I could already hear the sounds of the shadow-creatures moving nearby, sniffing the air as if searching for me.

The darkness was total by that point, and night had settled insidiously over the world without my notice. At some point it was day, and then it was night.

I closed the door of the gas station shut behind me, terrified of the complete lack of protection it offered. The top half of the glass had been shattered, making the process of locking it a pointless effort. Nonetheless, I did so, turning the lock and wincing at the loud sound of it snapping shut.

Sitting behind the counter where the cash register had once sat, I waited for the creatures outside to hopefully pass by. But I knew there was a good chance they had seen me or heard me, because they were known for their keen senses.

Not even a minute had passed by before I heard them outside, only a few feet away.

Their feet crunched across the same shattered glass I had walked on moments prior. A sound of sniffing could be heard, and husky breathing. I froze in place, too terrified to move, and then a deep, guttural voice began to whisper.

No one had ever heard the creatures speak before, to my knowledge. But these ones were talking back and forth between each other in low, rumbling voices.

I held my breath, waiting in the darkness, shivering and praying that they would go past.

But then a moment later they were inside.

Pitch-black shadow shapes grabbed me roughly and pulled me up from the ground. They covered my mouth with something wet and sticky like slime, so I was unable to speak, and began to carry me away from the gas station.

I tried to make out the details of these creatures in the low light of the moon, but could see very little. I caught glimpses of rough, wiry fur - dark and thick. Their eyes reflected golden in the night, and their teeth were sharp and pointed, meant for ripping flesh from bone.

No matter how hard I tried to scream, nothing made it through the gunk which they had used to cover my mouth, like tarry mud. It seeped into my mouth every time I opened it, and I reminded myself to keep it shut.

My heart was hammering with fear as their cold, slimy hands clasped my arms, carrying me away against my will. I was thrashing and kicking, but they held firm and continued dragging me away from the gas station, through the trees into the forest.

Eventually I had no choice but to accept my fate. Whatever these things were, they were going to kill me and consume me, maybe not in that order.

The creatures brought me to a cave. Taking me inside with them, they brought me down deeper and deeper into tunnels which were winding and narrow, and sometimes through caverns as large as football stadiums. But every movement they made seemed planned and orchestrated, as if they were following a set route.

Deeper down into the darkness we went, and I barely caught a glimpse of my captors, as they muttered back and forth in an unknown language, low and rumbling like gravel being poured.

After a long, long time, I actually fell asleep. I couldn't help it. We'd been traveling for so long, what felt like hours, and the adrenaline rush had passed and with it I'd been overcome with a need for sleep so deep I could not deny it.

When I awoke, it felt like a full night had passed, and my nightmares were quickly forgotten as I jumped to my feet and looked around. I was not in a cage or chained to a wall. Instead the creatures had left me free to wander around when I woke up.

The things were all around me, looking at me as if curious what I would do.

They stood on two legs and watched me with intelligent, passive eyes. Despite carrying me here against my will, they looked peaceful now.

I took in the place around me and found to my surprise that it was warm down here, and there was light coming from somewhere. It was shimmering a dull green glow, and I tried to figure out where it was coming from but couldn't.

"It's a geothermal heat source," a voice said from behind me.

I jumped with fright and backed away, turning around to see a man was behind me, his hands held upright in a peaceful gesture. There were other people too, I saw. Dozens of them were down here, living with the creatures.

"We've been trying to figure out how it works, and if we can bring it to the surface."

The man came a bit closer, but kept a respectful distance.

"What are they?" I asked nervously.

"We can't communicate with them much yet. But we know a little bit more than we did at first. We believe they are a branch of human evolution which went underground following a meteor event and subsequent ice age. They chose not to return to the surface, and instead they stayed in the deepest caves and in the darkness. Waiting for the world to freeze over again - which it has now, in a way."

I remembered seeing a map once, which showed the cave systems of the USA overlaid with all the missing persons cases. The two overlapped perfectly, indicating that wherever these cave systems existed, many people went missing, just like I was missing now. Were these cave people responsible all along?

"What do they want from us? Why did they bring me here?"

He looked around nervously, then came a bit closer before speaking under his breath.

"They think they are helping us by bringing us down here. When people escape it angers them greatly, as if we are giving up a sacred gift they've given us."

"I guess in a way it is a gift," I said, considering this. "It's warm down here. It's safe. There's light and heat. Do they have food? Maybe they'll let me bring my wife down here."

"Don't get too excited. Personally, I want out. You might want to see what they're offering up for dinner before you commit to staying. If you want to go with me, I'm leaving at first light. I've got the path all mapped out."

I shook the man's hand right then and there.

"Deal," I said. "Thanks. My name's Jordan. What's yours?"

"David," he said. "Come on, I think they're about to serve our evening meal. You might not be hungry when you see it, though."

*

A cold stone slab had been set up as a table in the underground cavern, and the kidnapped people and humanoid creatures assembled around it, most standing up while a few sat down on rocks.

And then two large sacks were brought into the room and their contents were emptied out on the stone slab. There were a few dead bats and mice, rats and other critters, but mostly it was an assortment of bugs. Millipedes and worms, spiders and potato bugs, beetles and roaches, still living, squirming, crawling, and trying to escape.

The humanoid creatures began to devour everything, first going for the bats and stripping their bodies of their hairy flesh, then going on to the rats and mice next. The hot smell of blood rose up in the air, the sewage-stink of entrails following after it.

One of the creatures saw me looking stunned and mistook the expression on my face for hunger, since it grabbed a handful of intestines and held it out to me. I took it, slightly worried what it would do if I refused.

I snuck away from the stone slab and found David. He was not eating, I noticed. He couldn't stomach the menu in this place either, I guessed.

"Let me know when you leave," I said. "I'm going with you."

*

The two of us left the cavern after everyone else had gone to sleep.

Following a twisting series of tunnels, we ascended up and up, walking for nearly a full day. But finally we reached the surface. I breathed in a deep intake of fresh air, and was glad to be outside again, despite the cold. The sun was low in the sky and I guessed it was getting dark soon.

"Thank you," I said, waving as we went our separate ways. "I hope our paths cross again, David. I really need to run. Literally."

"Hang on," he called after me. "I don't usually do this. You don't know who you can trust these days. But… Did you want to come back with me to my camp for tonight? It's close. And who knows, maybe we can set up a trade deal or something between our group and yours."

I hesitated, but the more I considered it the more I decided I should go with him. If I didn't go now that would ruin any chances of a partnership. And we needed all the help we could get.

"Okay," I said. "Lead the way. But I need to get home before dark. Is your camp far from here?"

"Not far at all. Just a half mile north. Come on, we can be there before dusk if we run."

The two of us found the road where I had first been captured, and I saw the gas station a little ways away. Then I was startled to see a figure in the road. Even from a distance I could tell who it was.

It was Sarah, my wife. And she looked hurt.

I ran towards her and when I got closer I saw her clothing was torn and she was covered in gashes and claw marks, her face black and blue with bruises.

"What happened!?" I yelled, taking her in my arms.

"It was the creatures. They attacked our camp. Gregory, Cathy, Jason… Everyone is dead. They killed everyone."

"What? How?"

This made no sense to me. I thought I'd just seen the truth about the creatures. They weren't evil. It was actually just a group of underground cave people, trying to help people in their strange way. I tried to tell Sarah that, but David interjected.

"No, no, no… I'm sorry to interrupt but you should know - the creatures are very real. You just got lucky the cave people found you first. Otherwise you definitely would have died out here the other night. Those things are out of control. They're practically invisible, but they're everywhere. Huge, eight-legged monsters that can blend in with the shadows and crawl up behind you silently in an instant."

The sun was almost setting now. It was getting very dim outside.

"We need to go," I said. "This is David. He said we could go with him to his camp, I think we should go with him. The cave people are… another option… But personally I say we go with him."

Sarah looked shell-shocked and completely broken from everything that had happened. She simply shook her head.

"You decide. I'll go wherever you think is best."

I decided to go with David. A decision that I would come to soon regret.

He brought us to an old, abandoned mall. Immediately that made me feel nervous, since most people avoided buildings like that. They were too big to control. Too open and unguardable.

"This is where you guys are living?" I asked dubiously.

"Just temporarily," he said. "It's not ideal, I know. But we found a good spot in the basement that we can easily guard. Only one way in and out."

We followed him inside and I looked over to see my wife eyeing the surroundings nervously. I gripped her hand tightly and proceeded forward on wobbly legs, following after the man.

He looked back occasionally to see if we were still following, giving a slightly creepy smile which grew wider each time.

Finally, we reached the stairs to the basement, and he led us down into the darkness. I saw there were no lights on down there, and my heart immediately began to jackhammer with fear.

I remembered the stories I had heard of people who lived symbiotically with the shadow creatures, luring people to their nests in order to feed them, in exchange for safety.

"It's not much further," David said, and I saw something glowing in his pocket.

Reaching down to grab it, I pickpocketed the man who was luring us to our deaths, and grabbed the hunk of rock he had stolen from the caves. Amazingly, it was warm to the touch! And it glowed a soft, pale green color, just like the ones in the underground caverns. It was a little piece of that place which this man had stolen and brought to the surface for himself.

But now it was mine. That was the price he'd have to pay for trying to kill us.

I kicked him down the remaining stairs as I saw shadowy spider legs beginning to emerge from the darkness, and I grabbed my wife's hand, yelling at her to run.

"NO!" David screamed tumbling down to the bottom of the stairs, his right leg broken and bent at an unnatural angle. Blood poured out from his mouth and one ear. "You can't leave me here with them! They can smell blood!"

The shadow creatures were on him a second later, devouring him as he screamed. I risked one quick glance over my shoulder to see if they were following us, and wished I hadn't.

*

Sarah and I made it out of that mall and marked the doors with an "X" to show it was a nest for the creatures.

We ran to the nearest shelter and hid. And we survived that night, against all odds.

The little chunk of glowing rock which I stole from David, whatever it is, carries with it a sense of hope. It's warm, and it lights up our new home in the darkest hours of night. Even when we're at our lowest.

We lost our old family. Everyone from our camp is gone. Everyone we knew is dead.

But we're starting a new tribe.

Sarah is just beginning to show. And I wonder if it'll be a boy or a girl.

Either way, I'll be happy.

Maybe being alive isn't so bad after all.

Maybe we can survive.

In a world without fire.

The Wolf of Skinwalker Ranch

My wife and I were sitting on the front porch after a long day of moving furniture and boxes into our new house.

We were tired, red-faced, and sweating after sharing the burden between the two of us. The sun was setting on the horizon as we sipped our warm beers and looked out over the landscape of our newly-acquired ranch.

Fields stretched off into the distance as far as the eye could see, not a neighbour in sight for miles. The cows were grazing, looking unhappy, their tails hanging straight down as they ignored the fresh grass all around them. I figured they were just upset from the long move.

"Why do you think they needed so many locks?" my wife asked, taking a sip of her beer. It was the elephant in the room, so to speak, and I had to admit I was curious about it as well. Every door in the house had a deadbolt on it, inside and out. Not only that, but the windows were shielded by thick iron bars. The old owners had left long before we could ask them about it.

"The folks who lived here before were probably paranoid about home invasions so far from the city. We'll take them down and I'll fill the screw holes with wood putty. We'll paint them over and they'll be good as new. You wanted to redo the trim anyway."

"And the bars on the windows?"

"That'll take a bit more work, but I can get it done before the weekend. I'll just have to run over to the hardware store to grab a few things. I can't find some of my tools - maybe they got lost during the move."

My wife was no longer paying attention. She was staring at some point far off in the distance.

"What's that?" she asked, pointing.

I followed her finger and looked to see a large grey wolf moving in the fields. It seemed to be stalking deliberately toward us, marching at a steady, quick pace.

It came to a fence and did the strangest thing. Instead of leaping over it, or burrowing under it, as I'd expected, it stood up on two legs like a person, grasped the loose corner of the wire fencing, and pulled it up, ducking between the strands and stepping through, one leg after the other. It was exactly how I would have done it.

Once it was on the other side it went back on four legs and started its progress toward us again. Then it looked up and saw us staring at it.

The grey wolf stayed still for a few seconds, then disappeared in the tall grass suddenly. It was just gone. It didn't dive into the grass or duck down - it was there, and then a moment later it was just gone. Vanished in the blink of an eye.

The two of us sat uneasily on the porch and I stood up to look in the distance, trying to spot the creature. But it was nowhere to be found.

"I'm going inside. You should come too," my wife said, sounding nervous.

We went in and locked the doors at the front and back of the house. The bars stayed on the windows after that, and my wife didn't mention the deadbolts on the doors in the house again either.

The two of us went to bed that night with little talk between us - a big difference from the ecstatic chatter that had been the norm all day prior to the event with the wolf. Or whatever that thing was. I got the feeling "wolf" was not quite the right word.

*

That night something else even more disturbing happened to us both.

I woke up in the early hours of the morning - around 3:30AM according to the bedside alarm clock. When I looked next to me in the bed and saw my wife's spot was empty, I became immediately concerned for her safety. Where could she have gone at this time of night, I wondered?

That was when I heard her voice calling to me from outside the window, asking insistently for me to let her in. Her cries for help were muffled through the glass and I lifted the heavy old windowpane up to hear her better.

"What are you doing out there?" I asked, worried about the wolf we'd seen earlier. I was looking around for glowing eyes reflecting the moonlight nearby. Standing on two legs or four, I wasn't sure which to expect.

"I must have been sleepwalking," she said dreamily. "The front door locked behind me somehow. You have to let me back in. Please. It's cold out here."

"I'll be right down," I said, without thinking about how impossible all of that was. I was only concerned for her safety at that moment. And she had been known to sleepwalk occasionally, so that part seemed to make sense.

I raced down the stairs in my boxers and grasped the front door knob in my hand, turning it. Thankfully, it was locked, or who knows what might have happened. Reaching up to turn the lock I was startled to hear a voice behind me.

"What are you doing?" my wife asked. I jumped at the sound, my heartbeat quickening. But what terrified me even more was what I had just seen outside. Given the timeframe it had taken me to get downstairs, it was impossible that it had been her. It was like someone else had been out there, wearing her skin and speaking in her voice.

Looking at the woman standing in front of me, I had no doubt it was Christine, my wife. Panting, I walked over to her and hugged her tightly.

"What's wrong?" she asked.

I didn't answer, afraid she would think I was losing my mind. Some things we don't share with anyone, not even our significant others. We take them to our grave, afraid that if we speak of them out loud it will make them true, and it will make the source of the impossible things return.

So instead I just took her hand and led her up the stairs, looking back nervously over my shoulder at the front door, waiting for the sound of a key turning in the lock. Or the sound of it being broken down by powerful forces beyond my control.

Instead, there was a gentle knock. Polite almost, at first.

But then the fist began to pound against the front door of the house louder and louder, more and more insistently. My wife stopped, turning around to look at me on the stairs.

"Who could that be at this time of night?" she asked.

"Just ignore it. Let's go to bed. They'll go away… eventually."

After a few moments of hesitation she turned around and began going up the stairs once more, taking a couple nervous looks back as she did. We kept walking up the stairs as the pounding continued, devolving into steady scratching noises that didn't cease until daybreak.

*

"What were you doing down in the basement last night?" my wife asked at the breakfast table the next morning. Neither one of us mentioned the sounds at the door the night before. We were both trying to act like it had never happened. In the light of the morning it seemed like a shared hallucination. A bad dream brought on by warm beer and too much time spent moving boxes without enough assistance.

"In the basement? I wasn't in the basement," I told her.

"Yeah you were. You were calling my name, asking me to come down there."

I looked at her with concern.

"When was this?"

"Right before I found you at the front door. I figured I just missed you, that you found whatever you were looking for down in the basement and went into the kitchen for a snack or something. But then I found you by the front door."

"I was never in the basement last night…"

She looked at me, puzzled.

"Of course you were. Who else would have been calling for me from down there?"

I debated telling her what I had seen outside and decided I probably should. We were clearly dealing with something very strange here and we needed to be on the same team if we were going to figure it out.

"Christine, did you go outside at all last night?"

"No… What does that have to do with-"

"Okay. So, here's the thing. I saw you outside. At the same time when you were going down to the basement. You were calling to me from out front, saying you had been sleepwalking and you were locked out. That's why I was at the door. I never went down to the basement and I don't think that was really you outside, either. I think there's something else causing all this to happen."

"What the hell could cause THAT to happen!?"

I opened my mouth to answer when there was a polite rapping at the door. The two of us sat dead silent for a few moments, unsure what to do.

The knocking came again, and I heard a man's voice, muffled through the door, saying, "There's a car here. Maybe they're out in the fields."

"Should we just leave it on the doorstep?" a woman's voice asked.

"I don't like being here any more than you do, but that seems a bit rude. Maybe we should come back."

Christine and I both stood up, sensing that this was not the same entity from the night before. I don't know how I could tell, but I just could. This wasn't an evil presence, it was just some neighbours coming by to welcome us. And they sounded like they might know something more than we did about the ranch and its mysteries.

I opened the front door and saw a man and woman with their backs turned, walking away from us. They spun around when they heard the sound of us opening up.

"Oh, hi there! We're the Turnbulls! We live down the road. Technically next door, as if there is such a thing out here. But we do share an easement with you to access the river... Jack takes the cattle down that way sometimes for a change of scenery."

The man put his arm around his wife's shoulder and whispered something in her ear. She abruptly stopped talking, realizing that she was rambling on nervously.

"Sharon, I'm sure they don't want to get into all that. We just wanted to stop by and welcome you to the neighbourhood, so to speak. It's nice to have another couple living next door again. This place has been empty for so long…"

My wife and I looked at each other with surprise. As far as we knew the place had been occupied right up until our arrival. It hadn't shown signs of disrepair or neglect, so we'd had no reason to think otherwise.

"Really? No wonder the place was such a bargain. How long was it empty for?"

The man and woman shared a look.

"Oh, you know… Not *that* long. A few years. Anyways, we just wanted to bring this casserole. We have a few errands to run, but it was great meeting you both. Come on by our place anytime, we're number 56981, the next driveway on your side, up that way," the man said, hooking his thumb eastward. I had never seen anyone introduce themselves and run so quickly. I tried not to take it personally.

"It was so nice to meet you both," the woman said, taking a few quick steps towards my wife and handing her the casserole dish. "You can keep that dish, by the way. It's Pyrex. Great for casseroles."

She backed up to join her husband, looking around the property nervously as she did.

"Hey, can I ask you something?"

The two of them looked ready to run back to their car, but they stopped and nodded, shifting on their feet anxiously and waiting for me to speak.

"Have you ever seen anything... Uh, how should I put this? There's been a couple weird occurrences since we moved in and I was just wondering if you could tell us anything? Is this place haunted? Is that why it was so cheap? I can tell you guys are nervous. Just give us something to work with. Please. We're getting a little freaked out."

The woman looked pleadingly at her husband. He nodded to her and she went back to the car and got in the passenger seat where she sat darting her eyes around from side to side.

"What exactly did you see?" the man asked. "Wait, no. Don't tell me. It's better if we don't speak of them. They know when you talk about them. It's better if we don't."

"Well then, how do we get rid of them?"

"You don't. These things have been around a lot longer than you or me. My wife and I get our share of strange events on the ranch next door too, but not as bad as here. This place... Well, there's something here that makes it special. And not in a good way, I'm sorry to say. I'd tell you more, but it would only make things worse. It always does."

There was a sound of knuckles rapping against the glass and I looked to see his wife banging on the car window, looking with wide eyes at us and pointing into the distance, towards the fields.

My eyes followed where she was pointing and I looked to see the large grey wolf was back. And it was moving towards us again.

"I told you. We're not meant to speak of them. I need to go. The two of you should decide soon if you want to stay. This place will change you. And it will take things from you. You only get so long to decide. If you wait to see what the changes will be, it will already be too late. Trust me."

With that he turned away and went back to his car. He started the engine and drove off much quicker than I would have thought safe on the dirt driveway, swerving and leaving a cloud of dust hanging in the air around us, obstructing my view for a few seconds.

When I turned around again, the wolf was much, much closer.

It was about fifty yards away and closing in fast. It was looking at me intently. My wife was running back towards the house, yelling at me to come, but I was frozen, watching the wolf as it stood on its hind legs again.

Not a wolf. Stop calling it a wolf. It's not a wolf. It's just trying to fool you into thinking that's what it is. But it's so much more dangerous than that.

I tried to take a step but my legs wouldn't budge. My eyes were locked on the wolf as it began to stalk towards me, no longer an animal but something else wearing an animal suit. The ancient leathery skinned humanoid beneath the wolf armor could be glimpsed occasionally as it strode like a hunter in my direction, taking long steps, moving low to the ground. The fur pieces were simply strapped onto it like clothing, the wolf head strapped on like a hat.

"WHAT ARE YOU DOING!? GET IN HERE!" my wife yelled one more time and my foot suddenly started to move.

As soon as it did I found I was unfrozen and finally able to start running, and not a second too soon. The house was close, but the thing was fast. When it saw me beginning to run, it became a wolf again in an instant.

The idea that it was anything but that seemed ludicrous as I watched it race towards me on all fours, its snapping jaws dripping saliva as it dove to cut me off. This thing was a massive grey wolf, through-and-through. It could be nothing but that. And yet my eyes had begged otherwise just a moment before.

If not for my wife it might have gotten me. But she saw what was happening and took a large rock we had been using as a doorstop and threw it straight at the thing's head.

It missed, hitting the beast in the shoulder instead, but it was enough to drive it back for a brief second. Which was all I needed. I ran into the house and slammed the door shut behind me. An instant later the scratching began again. Soon there was another one at the back door, scratching it as well. The sounds continued for hours.

When the noises stopped and I finally ventured outside again, I found that three of the cattle had been killed. The others were scared out of their wits, hiding huddled together in a corner of the field near to the house. Their eyes darted around the fields, reminding me of how the neighbours had looked, as they scanned our property for the things lurking in the shadows.

I was beginning to suspect we were not going to be able to stay in this place much longer. Even if we could survive, this was no way to live.

That night, my wife and I sat in the living room with all the blinds and curtains drawn, discussing what we would do. The house wouldn't sell quickly, that much was obvious based on the neighbours' statements. The two of us decided we would leave in the morning, regardless. We would stay in a motel until we found an apartment to rent, sacrificing all of our investment in the house. Even if we put it up for sale again it would be a long, long time before we made any portion of our money back. But it was too dangerous and too terrifying to stay.

"I'm going to bed," my wife said, looking tired. "Come upstairs soon, okay? I don't want to be alone."

"I'll be up in a minute," I told her. "I just want to grab a glass of water."

She nodded sleepily and went up the stairs slowly, looking depressed. We had dreamed about this move for so long, and now it was all coming to ruins. I felt sad about it too.

I went into the kitchen and poured a glass of water. After drinking it down in one long gulp I decided I needed another.

It had been a long day and I'd been too distracted to drink anything.

A noise came from upstairs. A scraping sound like claws.

Setting down the glass, I turned around and listened closely.

"Christine?"

She didn't reply.

I took a few steps across the linoleum floor of the kitchen before calling out again. Once again there was no answer.

By the time I got to the bottom of the stairs my heart was pounding so fast and hard I felt like it would beat right out of my chest. I opened my mouth to call her name one more time when I saw it.

The wolf that wasn't a wolf strode on two legs across the gap at the top of the stairs, then disappeared around the corner, heading towards my wife. It was so quick that I thought for a moment I could have imagined it. Just a grey blur that was gone in an instant. If not for the fact that it looked down the stairs at me and smiled, its long canines gleaming in the light. Its eyes were pure blackness.

I ran up the stairs as fast as I could, terrified of what it would do to her.

When I got to the second floor, I looked down the hall to see all of the doors were closed. It was as if the whole thing had really been just my imagination.

Taking an unsteady step towards the bedroom, my heartbeat did not slow down even slightly. My hand was shaking as I reached for the door knob, turning it and entering the master bedroom.

I entered hesitantly, finding the room dark and my wife asleep in bed. Part of me wanted to wake her up, but for some reason I didn't.

It will be fine, just go to bed, my irrational thoughts said. My pounding heart began to slow and my eyelids grew heavy.

This is fine, my mind told me. Everything is fine. Just go to sleep now.

Trying not to think of what I had seen just moments before, I climbed into bed, getting in next to my wife and shivering while my body warmed up beneath the sheets.

There was a soft sound of padding footsteps outside the bedroom door.

Scratch, scratch, scratch

Something wants to get inside the bedroom.

And a strange, foreign voice in my mind is telling me to let it in.

I Sat Next to a Strange Man on the Plane

We had reached cruising altitude and the passenger airplane I was sitting aboard was sailing turbulently through the sky, riding on air currents and exploiting physics in ways that I would never understand.

Maybe it was my ignorance of these principles which made me so nervous - my legs trembling with constant vibrations. My teeth had even been chattering for a while during takeoff. But now my nerves had settled down to a dull roar.

"Are you sure you're alright?" the white-haired man sitting next to me asked, his hand settling on my arm in a comforting way. "Should I call the stewardess over? She can get you some water, or a cup of tea to calm the nerves? With a shot of brandy too, maybe?"

He laughed, gripping my arm just a little *too* firmly now.

"I'm fine," I said. "The worst of it's passed. As long as we don't run into engine trouble I should be okay."

That statement prompted angry glares from passengers nearby, who quickly went back to reading or talking amongst themselves. I scolded myself internally for saying my worst fears out loud. Nobody liked to think of engine trouble when they were flying over the Atlantic Ocean late at night.

"Well, let's not speak of those things just now. Do you want a book to read? I brought a spare novel. It's a John Grisham."

"No, thanks."

"Well, how about some television? I think they have cable on these little things nowadays." He pointed at the screen on the headrest in front of me. I hadn't even noticed it there.

"That's a good idea. Maybe I'll find something distracting"

I turned the power on and noticed immediately the lack of sound. Of course, I had forgotten to bring earphones.

"Here," the man next to me said, handing me a pair of his own. "I'm not using them right now. You can borrow them."

They were the kind with foam pads on the outside of the headphones, not earbuds, so I felt relatively safe using them, even though I am a bit of a germaphobe. At least we wouldn't be swapping earwax.

"Thanks," I said, taking them and putting them on, plugging the cord into the headphone jack. A squeal of feedback caused me to recoil, and I turned the volume down, finding it had been set to maximum.

The man was speaking again and I pulled back the headphone to hear him better.

"Anything I can do to help. I used to have a terrible fear of flying – but after you do it a few times you get used to it."

I smiled weakly, feeling nauseated from not eating. I hadn't been able to stomach breakfast that morning or any other meal for that matter. It had been over 24 hours since I'd eaten or slept, due to my nerves about flying.

Putting the earphones back on, I began to flip through the channels on the little television set in front of me.

Discovery Channel came on and I decided to leave it there. It was a show about the Amazon Rainforest, describing ancient civilizations which had resided in the jungles. Using new technology, they had found the outlines of massive cities, which had housed millions of ancient Amazonians. Their gods and their myths, lost over hundreds of years.

I was watching this as the man sitting next to me began to remove something from his bag. It was a tupperware container with a bright red lid on top.

He opened the lid and an odor more foul than anything I had ever experienced wafted out, hitting me in the face like a punch to the nose. It smelled like old, rancid seafood. Like a dumpster which has been sitting open in the hot sun, full of used diapers and bad shrimp.

The man produced a fork from his bag and lifted the container to his nose, closing his eyes as he savored the smell. Using his hand like a fan, he waved more of the stink towards his face, like a gourmand about to eat a Michelin star meal.

Despite my disgust, I couldn't help but steal a glance at what was in the container. It looked like a fish had been tossed in a food processor, bones and all, only it hadn't been blended for long enough. There were still obvious pieces of bone, scales, and a fish head could be seen left partially intact. A bulging white eyeball was prominent among the pieces. He dug in his fork and took a large bite, going for the eyeball first. I heard it squish between his teeth and explode in his mouth. Black, viscous fluid dribbled down his chin, landing on his shirt.

I couldn't believe nobody was complaining about the smell. Nobody else seemed to even notice, except for me. If not for how nice he had been to me, I would have said something. The stink was really making me feel sick.

He saw me looking and dug his fork into the mess, then held out a large, heaping bite for me. I could practically see the stink lines coming off of it, like a cartoon skunk.

"Did you want to try some?" he asked, his yellowed teeth showing as he smiled.

That grin, somehow predatory and leering, made me second-guess everything about the man. Suddenly he didn't seem nice anymore. He was mocking and cruel - his previous niceties just a facade to hide his true nature. And what an actor he was!

"No thanks," I said, gulping down a lump of bile in my throat, trying to force a smile but failing miserably. "I just ate before the flight."

He looked at me as if staring directly into my soul. Then he shook his head, as if saying no, like he didn't believe me. He sucked his teeth and went back to his meal.

"You shouldn't lie to me, you know."

I pretended not to hear that and went back to looking at the television, trying to distract myself from the scene happening next to me. But my heart was thumping fast now and I could feel a throbbing pulse in my jugular.

The Amazon history show was finished and now something else was on. It was a show about aviation disasters. And how planes malfunction before crashing. A voice-over was speaking about horrible tragedies and near-misses, showing computer generated images illustrating the critical parts of the airplane which had broken. Then they switched to the passenger footage which had been recorded on people's phones during troubled flights.

"During this Air Asia flight, severe turbulence caused the hospitalization of more than five passengers, as the plane was eventually rerouted to Tokyo…"

The screen showed images of a plane's interior, shuddering up and down violently and sending people flying into the ceiling and into the aisles. Women and men could be heard screaming as luggage cascaded from overhead compartments and people prayed for safety.

"I was on that flight," the man next to me said, licking his gore-smeared fingers clean. "One hell of an in-flight meal, let me tell you."

I tried turning off the television, but it didn't work. I tried to change the channels, but that button was broken too. It was stuck on this particular program, and there was no way to get rid of it. Instead, I tore the headphones off and unplugged them, handing them back to the man.

"You don't want to watch it anymore?" he asked, slurping up some of the roadkill casserole.

"No. Thanks for letting me use your headphones. I think I'm just gonna try to take a nap."

"Suit yourself," he said, crunching a bone between his teeth. "I'll wake you up for meal service."

How he could still be hungry was a mystery to me, after he had just ingested such a monstrous dinner.

I was already beginning to suspect there was something off about this man. The way he had changed was unsettling, and I felt like I was suddenly in the Twilight Zone. He just wasn't acting normal.

So I watched him out of the corner of my eye for a while, trying to convince myself he was just a bit odd, and nothing to worry about. He was just an eccentric with a very unusual diet. Eventually I managed to convince myself that was true, and despite my unease, my tiredness won over everything else and I fell asleep.

I didn't remember my dreams, only waking up to find myself completely alone on the plane.

The hateful man sitting next to me was gone and so was everyone else. The plane was still rumbling turbulently through the air, but now with no one in it. I looked outside and saw the sky was clear and bright blue, and was no longer night.

But we were flying towards a dark thunderhead, booming with lightning up ahead in the distance. The storm-front looked to be ten miles high and a thousand miles wide - a swirling, dark mass of angry weather. A Category Fucked hurricane that could take out a city without warning.

I stood up and looked around the plane, still not understanding how it could be empty. Where had everyone gone? How long had I been out? Had they allowed me to sleep right through deplaning?

Before I had another moment to think, the plane bounced up and down with a sickening yo-yo motion, then careened to the side. It did this a few more times, in rapid succession, pitching forward and backward so that I was thrown off balance and sent tumbling into the aisle.

By the time it settled again, I wanted to puke. But at least the plane had leveled out again.

I stood up from the floor and glanced out the window. I saw we had just passed into the massive thunderhead, and the inside of the plane was suddenly pitch black.

There was a voice whispering from all around me, speaking my worst fears aloud. Black, inky tendrils like smoke began to reach out towards me from the shadows.

"You're alone. The plane is going down."

"It will sink. In the middle of the ocean."

"Freezing. Drowning. Water in your lungs."

"Falling, dropping, plunging from the sky."

"You know you're going to die."

I stumbled forward down the aisle, moving towards the cockpit. They needed to turn this plane around. How did they not see it? The interior panels of the plane on both sides suddenly made loud, rending noises, as if the craft were beginning to break apart at the seams. The walls bent inwards, exposing the insulation, and a sound like a pop can slowly being crushed could be heard from all around me.

Thunder crashed loudly outside and the panels pulled apart further, until I could hear the howling wind and rain and saw it blowing into the cabin. Lightning flashed and I could see it through a gap in the side of the plane, which grew even wider before my eyes.

"It's going down!" I yelled, stumbling forward. "We're gonna crash!"

The plane dipped and climbed upwards in a sickening way as we hit another pocket of turbulence. My heart was in my throat, my stomach doing backflips, as I lurched down the aisle holding onto the backs of chairs for support.

Finally I managed to reach the door of the cockpit. There were no flight attendants or passengers that I could see, but there had to be someone flying this plane.

I began to hammer on the door, screaming at them to let me in.

"It's going down!" I screamed again and again.

I heard laughter coming from the darkness all around me as I yelled at the captain hiding behind his steel door.

Once again I found myself on the floor, being tossed around in the turbulence, as we hit another rough patch.

I put my hands over my head and tried to cover my face as the plane's fuselage began to come apart and the wings began to break free from the body.

Looking up, I saw the door to the cockpit was now open and there was no one sitting inside. The pilot and copilot seats were empty.

I staggered to my feet to right the controls as the moment I saw inside the cockpit, the plane began to plummet from the sky.

It went into a nosedive and I was once again thrown backwards into the aisle, this time by the force of multiple G's.

I was screaming when I opened my eyes and found myself staring up at the faces of dozens of anxious passengers all around me. The flight attendants looked less anxious and more upset, as I had just ruined their quiet flight with what probably appeared to be a total nervous breakdown.

To the other passengers it had appeared that I was sleeping, then collapsed into the aisle screaming about the plane crashing.

I would have believed it was just a nightmare too, if not for the bruises I would find all over myself. Bruises left from my time being tossed around by the turbulence on the plane.

Several concerned passengers and crew ushered me back to my seat, where I was momentarily left alone again with the old man and his yellow teeth and horrible appetite.

"You made quite a scene back there," he said, picking his teeth with a toothpick.

"It was so real," I muttered. "How did it feel so real?"

He didn't answer, instead he began to speak about another topic.

"Do you know what's funny about fear?" He asked.

The question was hypothetical, so I just looked at him and waited for his answer.

"The funny thing about fear - at least when it comes to you humans - is that it doesn't work well if it gets dumped on you all at once. You need to get scared, then feel like everything is okay, then you can get scared again even more. But you start to feel desensitized to it if it comes at you non-stop. That's why horror movies have highs and lows. Moments of buildup and tension before the jump-scare."

The man's belly was swollen and one of his shirt buttons popped off, flying into the seat in front of him and clicking loudly off the television screen embedded there. He looked full, fat, happy, and satisfied for the first time since I'd met him. As if he'd just eaten a huge meal.

Gears were turning in my mind as I looked into his glossy black eyes and began to understand who he was, or at least what his motivations were. Just as I suspected, he was not a man at all.

"Bright lad," he said, as if he'd just read my mind. "I had a feeling you'd figure it out."

"It was you. The voice in the empty plane. You made me think it was real, and then you fed on my fear. You dined on it like that disgusting shit in your tupperware container."

"Ah, but fresh is always better than leftovers. I thank you, though. I haven't had a meal like that in quite a while. Your terror was so deep and so strong. What happened to you, anyways?"

I winced as if slapped, remembering my parents. Somehow, I had a feeling he already knew about them. Why else would he ask? Maybe he wasn't as satisfied as he looked.

I hit the call button and waited for a stewardess to come over, then I asked her if I could switch seats. I told her I'd sit anywhere, as long as it wasn't next to the disgusting old man beside me. "I think he's a demon," I said. "Now, I know how that sounds, but hear me out…"

The flight attendant gave me a worried look, as did several other passengers sitting in the vicinity. She cleared her throat and leaned in, speaking under her breath in an attempt to salvage what was left of my pride.

"Sir… The seat beside you is empty. I've been watching you during this flight and there's been nobody sitting there. You've been alone, and to be frank, you've been talking to yourself quite a bit. It's starting to worry some of the other passengers."

I stammered something, looking at the old man, unable to turn away from his wrinkled face and yellow teeth, pulled up in a widening grin.

"It's my responsibility to alert the captain of this and have you returned home to America for a psychiatric evaluation. You've got bruises all over you and it's obvious you're not able to care for yourself properly based on your behaviour during this flight. You're a danger to yourself and possibly to others."

An Air Marshall was sitting nearby and stood up, removing a pair of handcuffs from his belt.

"I've heard enough. And I agree with your assessment, Miss. I appreciate your patience with this man. He's clearly unwell."

Despite my protests, which quickly turned to screaming, he handcuffed one of my wrists to my seat.

"Luckily this plane is on a return trip to America after a couple hours layover here. So we'll be back up in the air in no time."

The two of them walked away, leaving me alone with the fear-eating demon sitting next to me. His true form was slowly beginning to show through the cracking facade of his human appearance, and I could see the rotting hell flesh beneath.

"No, no, no! Please! Don't make me go back! I don't want to go back! I'll take a boat! Let me take a boat! Just anything but this plane! YOU NEED TO GET ME OFF THIS PLANE!"

"Don't worry," said the old man, drool cascading out from his lower lip. "They used to be scared of flying too. But, after a few times, you'll start to get used to it."

Manor House Publishng Inc.
www.manor-house-publishing.com
905-648-4797

www.ingramcontent.com/pod-product-compliance
Lightning Source LLC
Chambersburg PA
CBHW060416310726

48976CB00003B/1076